THE SURGEON'S FATHERHOOD SURPRISE
Jennifer Taylor

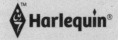

TORONTO NEW YORK LONDON
AMSTERDAM PARIS SYDNEY HAMBURG
STOCKHOLM ATHENS TOKYO MILAN MADRID
PRAGUE WARSAW BUDAPEST AUCKLAND

Special thanks and acknowledgment are given to Jennifer Taylor for her contribution to the the Brides of Penhally Bay series

Recycling programs
for this product may
not exist in your area.

ISBN-13: 978-0-373-06775-6

THE SURGEON'S FATHERHOOD SURPRISE

First North American Publication 2011

THE SURGEON'S FATHERHOOD SURPRISE

BRIDES OF PENHALLY BAY

Devoted doctors, single fathers, a sheikh surgeon, royalty, miracle babies and more…

Hearts made whole in an idyllic Cornish community

Last month Adam and Maggie were involved in a twenty-four-hour rescue mission where romance began to blossom as the sun started to set
The Doctor's Bride by Sunrise
by Josie Metcalfe

This month single dad Jack Tremayne finds a mother for his little boy—and a bride for himself
The Surgeon's Fatherhood Surprise
by Jennifer Taylor

And next month there's a princess in Penhally!
The Doctor's Royal Love-Child
by Kate Hardy

BRIDES OF PENHALLY BAY

A collection to treasure forever!

CHAPTER ONE

HAD it been a mistake to come back?

Jack Tremayne parked his car and switched off the engine. He sighed as he stared across the bay. The view was all too familiar. He had grown up in the small Cornish town of Penhally Bay and had lived here until he had gone away to med school. He had sworn that he would never return either, yet here he was, about to start a new life right back in the very place he had escaped from.

It had been two years since he had last visited the town and he hadn't missed it one little bit. There had been nothing here for him since his mother had died. His relationship with his father, Nick Tremayne, had always been a stormy one. Nothing Jack had done had ever been good enough for his father.

It had been almost as bad for his twin sister, Lucy, and his brother, Ed: they had never lived up to their father's overly high expectations for them either. However, it had been Jack who had borne the brunt of Nick Tremayne's displeasure, Jack who had rebelled against Nick's suffocating need to control his children's lives.

Leaving Penhally Bay had been the best thing Jack had ever done. Living and working in London had suited him perfectly. He had loved the buzz he'd got from working in the city as well as the opportunities it had afforded him to pursue a hectic social life. He would have happily remained there if life hadn't thrown up an unexpected obstacle.

Jack's gaze moved away from the view and he felt panic well up inside him as he glanced into the rear-view mirror. Little Freddie was fast asleep in his seat so that was a blessing. Jack had been dreading the long drive to Cornwall and it had been every bit as bad as he'd feared. Freddie had cried, non-stop, for hours before he had finally fallen asleep as they had been passing through Exeter.

Jack had felt so helpless as he had listened to him, but there again he'd felt helpless from the moment he had been told about Freddie. Finding out that he was a father had been a big enough shock, but to suddenly discover that he was solely responsible for the child's future had thrown him into a complete spin. How on earth was he going to manage to raise a child on his own?

He took a deep breath and opened the car door before he drowned in his own fear. Hunting the key out of his pocket, he unlocked the cottage door. The first thing on the agenda was to get Freddie inside and make him something to eat. Lucy had promised to stock the fridge, and a quick check of the kitchen showed that his sister had been as good as her word. There was even a casserole all ready and waiting for him to heat up. Brilliant! At least he wouldn't have to test out his decidedly shaky culinary skills.

Jack quickly unloaded the cases out of the boot and stacked them in the hallway. The cottage had been used as a holiday let for the past few years, and the furniture was pretty basic, but it would do for now. Once he got settled then he could think about furnishing the place properly—if he stayed, of course.

He groaned. He had to stop giving himself an escape clause. The only way he was going to be able to cope with fatherhood was if he had a lot of support, and the best person he could think of to help him was Lucy. Lucy would know what to do when Freddie woke up screaming in the night. She would know how to calm Freddie down when he started rocking backwards and forwards, locked into some terrifying world of his own. The psychiatrist Jack had consulted had explained that it would take time for the little boy to recover from the trauma he had suffered, and that was exactly what Jack intended to give him:time and a lot of love—if Freddie would let him.

His heart ached as he lifted the little boy out of the car and carried him indoors. Maybe he was hoping for too much, but he was desperate to forge some kind of a relationship with his son. At the moment Freddie tolerated him and that was all. If Jack hugged him or kissed him, Freddie didn't respond. He never laughed or smiled, only cried. It was as though the child's emotions had been switched off by the trauma of losing his mother in such terrible circumstances and, quite frankly, Jack had no idea how to switch them back on again.

After lying Freddie on the sitting-room sofa, Jack went into the kitchen and put the casserole in the oven. Lucy had left a note on the worktop to tell him what setting to switch the oven to and he grinned as he followed her instructions. Lucy was certainly under no illusions as to his culinary expertise!

He filled the kettle, then hunted a bag of coffee out of the cupboard and ripped it open, grimacing when a shower of grounds spilled onto the worktop. He was just looking for a cloth to wipe them up when there was a knock on the door and he smiled in delight. Lucy had promised to call round and he couldn't wait to see her and his new little niece.

'Hi! That was good timing,' he began as he opened the front door. He stopped abruptly when he saw the pretty blonde-haired woman who was standing on the pavement, smiling politely at him. He had no idea who she was but she definitely wasn't his sister.

'Sorry,' he apologised ruefully when he saw her smile waver. 'I thought you were someone else.'

'Lucy asked me to give you this.' She handed him a plastic container of milk. 'She's been held up at the surgery so she said to tell you that she won't be able to call round to see you until this evening.'

'Oh, right. Well, thanks for telling me. And thanks for this, too,' he added, holding up the milk.

'You're welcome,' she replied, and turned to leave.

Jack frowned as he stared after her retreating figure. He wasn't sure if it was something he'd said, but she had seemed in rather a hurry to get away. He'd had the distinct impression, in fact, that she had been eager not to engage him in conversation. How odd.

He was still puzzling it over as he went back inside. Freddie had woken up now so Jack hurried into the kitchen and poured him a beaker of milk. He took it back to the sitting room and crouched down in front of the sofa.

'Hey, tiger, how're you doing? Are you thirsty? Here you go.'

He handed the little boy the beaker, sighing as he saw how Freddie drew back into the corner of the sofa, as far away from him as possible. Still, at least he had stopped crying, and that was a definite improvement.

He went and checked on the casserole, which was hot enough by then to eat. He spooned it onto a couple of plates, found some cutlery and placed everything on the table, then went to fetch Freddie. However, as he helped the little boy onto a chair Jack felt the same sense of helplessness overwhelm him again. He was afraid that he wasn't equipped to be a father—afraid of making a mistake, afraid that he would make his son's life worse instead of better. All he could do was his best, but he was very aware that it might not be enough at the end of the day.

Just for a second his thoughts flickered back to the woman who had brought him the milk and he frowned. Obviously, she'd been less than impressed by him, too.

Stupid, stupid woman!

Alison Myers could feel her face flaming as she hurried along the road. She couldn't believe she had reacted that way when Jack Tremayne had opened the door. She'd had it all planned out, too—she would introduce herself, hand over the milk and pass on Lucy's message. Instead of which she'd ended up behaving like some sort of...of gauche teenager! What on earth had got into her? Was it the fact that the sight of Jack in the flesh had left her feeling so tongue-tied that it had been impossible to trot out all the usual pleasantries? Oh, please!

Alison was still berating herself when she let herself into the tiny cottage where she lived with her three-year-old son, Sam. It was ten minutes before five and she had a few minutes to spare before she needed to collect Sam from the childminder's house. Hurrying into the kitchen, she switched on the kettle and dropped a teabag into a mug. A cup of tea should help to settle her nerves, although it would take more than a cup of tea to rid of her of this embarrassment. Jack Tremayne must think she was the rudest person he had ever met!

Alison's hazel eyes darkened with mortification as she drank the tea. She knew that she was making far too much of what had happened but she couldn't help it. Jack Tremayne had become an almost legendary figure in her life. When she'd been going through the dark days following her divorce she had read a lot of magazines—the gossipy sort which ran stories about all the celebrities. Immersing herself in the tales of other people's lives had helped to take her mind off what had been happening in hers, and Jack had featured prominently in many of the stories. Pictures of him and his girlfriend, India Whitethorn—heiress to the multi-billion-pound Whitethorn Holidays empire—had been plastered over all the magazines.

Alison wasn't sure what it was about Jack that had appealed to her most—apart from the obvious, of course. Tall, dark, wickedly handsome and incredibly sexy, she couldn't have been the only woman who had made a point of looking out for him. However, it had been more than just his looks that had attracted her. Although he'd always seemed to be smiling in the photographs, there'd been a vulnerability about his expression that had touched a chord. She'd had a feeling that, despite all the glitz and the glamour that had surrounded his life, Jack had been far from happy. To her mind, at least, it had seemed as if there'd been a bond between them.

Alison groaned as she realised how ridiculous that was. She and Jack were poles apart! So maybe he had come back to Penhally Bay, but that had been out of necessity rather than choice, as Lucy had explained. Now that he had a son to care for—a child he had known absolutely nothing about, to boot—he'd decided that he needed his family around him. If it weren't for little Freddie, in fact, Jack would probably never have set foot in Cornwall again.

The thought was unsettling for some reason, but a quick glance at the clock soon drove it from her mind. Draining the last of her tea, Alison headed off to fetch Sam. There was nothing like a lively three-year-old to keep one's thoughts on track.

Jack had just settled Freddie down for the night when Lucy arrived. She grinned at him as she let her into the cottage.

'I never thought I'd see the day when you swopped the high life for domesticity, Jack,' she teased him, looking pointedly at the small T-shirt that was draped over his shoulder.

'Needs must, kiddo,' he drawled, giving her a bear hug.

Lucy hugged him back, then regarded him sternly. 'You are looking after yourself properly? I know how hard it is to look after a child, and fatherhood has never been exactly top of your agenda, has it? It would be all too easy to forget that you need to take care of yourself as well as Freddie.'

'Nag, nag, nag,' Jack muttered, grinning at her. 'You haven't taken your coat off yet and here you are, giving me a lecture.'

Lucy aimed a playful cuff at his ear. 'Just be thankful that someone cares about you, you ungrateful wretch!'

'I am. Honestly,' Jack said, with more feeling than he realised. He cleared his throat when he saw Lucy look at him. His sister was the only person alive who could get him to open up, but he wasn't sure if it was what he wanted to do. Apart from the fact that Lucy had her own family to think about now, he needed to take charge of his life.

He'd led a charmed existence in London. The parties, the premières, the dinners—as an eligible bachelor Jack had been inundated with invitations to all the top events, but now he had to move on, take responsibility for his son. The one thing he didn't intend to do was have the same kind of distant relationship with Freddie that his own father had with him.

It felt odd to realise how important that was to him. Jack summoned a smile, not wanting to share the thought even with Lucy. 'So how come you're on your own? I was hoping to get a look at my new little niece.'

'That was the plan, but then I ended up going into the surgery to help out.' Lucy took off her coat and dumped it over the back of the sofa. 'Dad got stuck at a call, and Dragan was called out too, so I offered to take the minor surgery clinic this afternoon.'

'Keeping your hand in?' Jack suggested, holding up the bottle of wine he'd opened. 'Fancy a glass?'

'I'd love one but I don't think Annabel will appreciate it. One of the drawbacks of breastfeeding. She gets to taste everything I do!'

Lucy grinned at him, her face alight with such happiness that Jack couldn't help feeling envious. It was obvious that his sister had taken to her new role as a mother like the proverbial duck to water, and he couldn't help comparing her attitude to India's. From what he had gathered, India had played at being a mother to Freddie as and when it had suited her. She had been more than happy to relinquish her responsibilities when she had grown tired of the role.

He pushed the thought aside because he didn't want to dwell on it. It upset him when he thought about what Freddie had been through, and it was pointless wishing that he had done something to prevent it. He had known nothing about the baby because India hadn't told him. She had simply used him to get pregnant. The only point in her favour was that she had left instructions with her solicitor that he should be told the truth in the event of her death.

A shudder ran through him at the thought that he might never have found out about Freddie if it weren't for that and he took a gulp of his wine. His emotions had been all upside down in the past few months, and it was scary to feel like this when he had always been in control of himself in the past.

'I don't know about keeping my hand in, but I did enjoy this afternoon,' Lucy admitted. 'I know Ben doesn't want me to rush back to work, but it was great to be back in the hustle and bustle for a couple of hours.'

'Maybe you could work part time?' Jack suggested. 'A couple of afternoons a month or something.'

'Hmm, that's what Alison suggested. Oh, she did remember the milk, I hope? I meant to get you some this morning but I forgot about it. Alison said she would drop some in on her way home.'

'Ah, so that's her name, is it? Alison.'

Jack swirled the wine around his glass as he tested out the name of the blonde-haired stranger. It suited her, he decided. She looked exactly how an Alison should look—sweet and feminine—even though she obviously hadn't judged him quite so favourably.

The thought stung a little, although he had no idea why it should have done, and he hurried on. 'I take it that she works at the surgery?'

'Yes. Didn't she say?' Lucy frowned when he shook his head. 'That's strange. Alison is usually very friendly. She's the practice nurse and all the patients adore her.'

'That's good,' Jack observed lightly, wondering what he'd done to get himself into Alison's bad books.

'We're really lucky to have her. She's a single mum— she has a little boy about the same age as your Freddie, in fact—so we try to tailor her hours to fit in with his needs.'

'What's her surname?' Jack asked, although it was a bit like poking at a sore tooth, trying to find out about this paragon who had taken such a dislike to him. He shrugged when Lucy looked at him in surprise. 'I was just wondering if I'd met her before. Is she local?'

'Yes, although she's not from Penhally Bay. Her surname is Myers. Her parents lived in Rock, I believe, although they're both dead now.' She sighed. 'She and her husband divorced not long after Sam was born so she's on her own. I don't envy her. It can't be easy being a single parent.'

'No, it isn't,' Jack agreed flatly.

Lucy grimaced. 'Sorry. I wasn't thinking. Anyway, you and Alison are completely different. After all, you have your family here to help you.'

'I have you,' Jack corrected her. 'I can't see Dad wanting to help out, can you?'

'You could be surprised,' Lucy assured him. 'He just adores Annabel. In fact, he's turning into a real doting grandfather!'

'I'm really glad about that, Lucy. I know that you and Ben had a tough time when you first got together again, so it's great that everything has turned out so well for you.'

'But you don't think Dad will feel the same about Freddie?'

He shrugged. 'I'll just have to wait and see.'

'I suppose so, but it could work out better than you think, Jack, especially now that you've moved back here. When do you start at the hospital?'

'Monday morning, bright and early.'

Jack dredged up a smile. There was no point getting cold feet at this point. He'd considered the drawbacks before he'd moved back to Penhally Bay and had decided they were outweighed by the pluses. Having Lucy around would help to get him through this really difficult period. And once Freddie had adapted to the changes in his life, then Jack could get himself back on track.

'I'm really looking forward to it, actually. My new boss has an excellent reputation and I'm hoping to learn a lot from her.'

'Great! At least one of us will end up as a top surgeon.' Lucy glanced at her watch and groaned. 'I'll have to go. Annabel will need feeding soon, and as she refuses to take a bottle I will have to be there otherwise Ben will be pulling his hair out.'

'It's been great to see you,' Jack said, helping her on with her coat.

'It has.' She hugged him tight, then grinned at him. 'See you very soon, big brother.'

'Good to hear you acknowledging my status,' Jack teased her. He was the older twin by ten minutes, a fact that he had reminded her about many times when they'd been growing up.

Lucy laughed. 'My big brother, the surgeon. Who could overlook your position in life, Jack?'

'Out before you say something you'll regret,' he retorted, shooing her out of the door.

Lucy paused on the step. 'I'll try to call round on Sunday with Ben and Annabel. In the meantime, if you need anything phone me. You have my number?'

'Yep.'

'And if there's anything really urgent that crops up, Alison lives just round the corner.' She pointed along the road. 'Number 2, Polkerris Road. Just knock on her door and I'm sure she'll do her very best to help you.'

'Fine,' Jack said, thinking that it would need a real, live emergency before he knocked on Alison's door. One rebuff was more than enough for any man if he hoped to salvage a scrap of his ego.

Lucy kissed him again, then ran to her car, waving out of the window as she drove away. Jack stood on the pavement after she'd left, listening to the sound of the waves crashing against the harbour wall. It was the very beginning of March and the air was cold and crisp, laden with salt and the smell of the sea. The scent was as heady as wine and he felt almost drunk on it after a couple of minutes.

He glanced along the road, his gaze lingering on the turning to Polkerris Road. Was Alison standing outside, taking in the view, or was she tucked up by the fire? He wasn't sure why he was interested in what she was doing, yet he was. For some reason he found it comforting to know that she was close by.

CHAPTER TWO

ALISON was on her way to bed when there was a knock on the front door. She hurried to answer it before Sam woke up. One of her neighbours had offered to lend her a DVD, and she assumed it was her, so it was a shock when she found Jack Tremayne standing outside. He was carrying a child all wrapped up in a blanket, and Alison frowned. What on earth was he doing, dragging his son out at this time of the night?

'I'm sorry to bother you, but you don't happen to have any analgesics suitable for a three-year-old, do you? I meant to stock up before I left London, but with one thing and another I completely forgot. The only thing I have to hand is aspirin and they're not at all suitable.'

'They most certainly aren't,' Alison replied. 'It's extremely dangerous to give a young child aspirin.'

'Yes, I know.'

Jack gave her a quick smile to show that he appreciated her advice, but she flushed. He was a doctor, for heaven's sake, and he didn't need her pointing out the dangers of dosing a child with the incorrect drugs. Opening the door wide, she stepped back.

'I've got some stuff which should help. Come in.'

'Oh, I didn't mean to disturb you…'

'You can hardly stand out there if your son is ill,' she

said, then immediately wished she hadn't said it in such a bossy tone of voice.

'Thanks.'

Jack's smile faded as he stepped inside the hallway. He paused politely, waiting for her to lead the way. Alison took him straight to the sitting room, because it was either that or the kitchen, and it didn't feel right to entertain Jack Tremayne in her cramped little kitchen.

'Sit down,' she invited, going over to the fireplace and poking at the embers. She added another log from the basket, replaced the guard and went to the door. 'I'll just fetch that bottle for you.'

'Thank you.'

Jack sank onto her sofa with a weary sigh. Alison paused when she realised how exhausted he looked. 'Are you OK?'

'Just about.' He gave her a tight smile as he glanced down at his son. 'I'll feel a lot better once this little chap is all right, though.'

Alison's heart immediately went out to him. She understood only too well how stressful it was when a child was ill. She smiled reassuringly at him. 'I'm sure Freddie will be fine. Let me get that medicine for you, then we can see if we can make him a bit more comfortable.'

Jack just nodded. He seemed too worn out to reply. Alison frowned as she made her way to the kitchen, because his response to Freddie being ill wasn't what she would have expected. The Jack Tremayne who had featured in all those magazine articles would have shrugged off the child's illness as something inconsequential, yet he appeared to be genuinely worried—*overly* worried, in fact.

She found the bottle of liquid analgesic, then took a measuring cup from the drawer and went back to the sitting room. Freddie was whimpering when she got back and Jack looked more worried than ever. Alison experienced a sudden urge to reassure him.

'Here you are. Shall I pour it while you hold him?' she offered, sitting down beside them.

'If you wouldn't mind.' Jack turned Freddie round so that he was facing her. 'Alison is going to give you some lovely medicine to make you feel better, tiger,' he crooned. 'Can you be a really brave boy and swallow it all down?'

Alison poured the correct dosage into the cup and offered it to the little boy, but he turned his head away. She smiled at him. 'It's really nice, Freddie. It tastes of strawberries—just try a little sip.'

She held the cup to his lips but he immediately flung back his head, catching Jack a glancing blow on the chin.

'Ouch!' Jack waggled his jaw from side to side, then grinned at his son. 'Good shot, tiger. That was nearly a knockout, and in the first round, too!'

Alison stood up, not wanting him to see how surprised she was by his reaction. She would have expected him to be annoyed by what had happened, but there'd been no trace of it in his voice. She hurried to the door, feeling guilty for having misjudged him.

'I'll make him a drink and pop this into it. Sam is never keen on taking medicine either, and I find it's easier to disguise it in some fruit juice.'

'We seem to be putting you to an awful lot of trouble,' Jack said ruefully.

'It's not a problem,' she assured him as she beat a hasty retreat. She went back to the kitchen and took a beaker out of the cupboard, realising that she should have asked if Freddie preferred orange juice or blackcurrant. She really didn't want to go back and ask, so she made up a drink of orange squash and added the medicine to it. She headed to the door, then paused and glanced at the kettle, wondering if she should make some tea while she was at it. It seemed very inhospitable not to offer Jack a drink.

She made a pot of tea and loaded everything onto a tray, then went back to the sitting room. Jack looked round when he heard her footsteps and grinned when he spotted the teapot.

'Don't tell me you're a mind-reader as well. I am absolutely dying for a cuppa.'

'Good.' Alison placed the tray on the coffee-table, then picked up the beaker and handed it to him. 'It's orange juice—I hope that's all right.'

'Fine. It's Freddie's favourite.' Jack handed the little boy the plastic cup, nodding in satisfaction when Freddie immediately began to gulp down the drink. 'Looks as though your plan has worked. I must remember it for future reference.'

'It's a lot easier than everyone getting stressed,' she assured him, kneeling down while she poured the tea.

'So it isn't just me who gets all worked up when his child is sick?'

Alison shook her head. 'No. Every parent is the same. It doesn't matter if you're a doctor or a dustman. You still worry yourself to death.'

'That's good to hear.' Jack reached for the mug and took a long swallow of the tea. 'Ah, that's better.'

Alison smiled as she picked up her own mug and sat down in the armchair. 'The cup that cheers, or so they say.'

'Well, whoever "they" are, they're quite correct. It's definitely cheering me up.' Jack took another drink from the mug, then put it down and laid his hand on Freddie's forehead. 'He seems to be cooling down a bit now, thank heavens.'

'Good. When did it all start?'

'I'm not sure. He was fine when I put him to bed, or as fine as he ever is.' He sighed as he settled the little boy, now sound asleep, more comfortably in his lap. 'He still hasn't adjusted properly. He misses his mother, and everything is so new and strange—even me. Especially me,' he added wistfully.

'Lucy said that you knew nothing about Freddie,' Alison said quietly.

'That's right. I didn't have a clue until India's solicitor phoned and asked me to go and see him.' Jack rested his head against the cushions and there was a look on his face that tugged at her heartstrings. 'I hadn't seen India since we'd split up. Oh, I'd heard on the grapevine that she'd had a baby, but it had never occurred to me the child might be mine.'

'Why do you think she didn't tell you?' Alison asked as she digested that.

'I don't know. I've racked my brain about it ever since I found out about Freddie, but I still don't know for sure why she didn't say anything to me. I can only assume that she wanted a baby but she didn't want all the rest.'

'The rest?'

'Marriage, commitment, the whole happily-ever-after scene.' Jack shrugged. 'A lot of India's friends were having children at the time, and I think she decided that she wanted a baby as well. I just happened to be around and able to fulfil her wish.'

'There must have been more to it than that!' Alison exclaimed.

'I doubt it. What India wanted, India got, and to hell with everyone else.'

Alison shivered when she heard the bitterness in his voice. Was Jack angry because India had taken the decision to have a child without consulting him? Or was he angry because of the position he now found himself in? It must have been a shock for him to have to take responsibility for his son. Looking after a child didn't exactly fit with the kind of hectic lifestyle Jack was used to. She could understand why he might be less than pleased by the change in his circumstances, even though her heart ached at the thought of his son suffering because of it.

'It isn't Freddie's fault,' she said defensively. 'You can't blame him for what his mother did.'

'I don't.' Jack looked at her in surprise. 'Freddie is the innocent victim of all this. When I think about what he must have been through…'

He stopped abruptly, his blue eyes clouding as he gently stroked the sleeping little boy's dark curls, and Alison felt something warm and tender well up inside when she saw the anguish on his face. Maybe it had been a shock for Jack when he had found out that he was a father, but he obviously cared about Freddie and that was something she admired. As she knew from her own experiences, not every man felt the same way.

She hurriedly pushed all thoughts of what had happened between her and Sam's father out of her mind. She had promised herself that she wouldn't allow herself to grow bitter and she intended to stick to that. 'Freddie's been through an awful lot. Losing his mother must have been very traumatic for him.'

'It was.' Jack glanced up and she saw the anger in his eyes. 'I don't know how much Lucy told you about what happened. I mean, it wasn't exactly a secret when all the papers carried the story.'

'Lucy hasn't said very much, but I read the reports. India died from a drug overdose, I believe?'

'That's right. She'd been dabbling in so-called recreational drugs for years. And before you ask, no, I never joined in. I'm not that stupid. She was clean when we were going out together so it was never an issue.'

Alison flushed when she heard the reprimand in his voice. 'I never thought you *had* taken them.'

'Oh, right. Sorry. So many people seem to assume that I was part of that scene as well, and it always gets to me.'

'Well, no one around here thinks that,' Alison assured him.

'Good.' He treated her to a smile, then carried on. 'According to the coroner's report, India suffered a massive heart attack after using cocaine. Maybe something could have been done to save her if there'd been anyone with her, but she was on her own when it happened. She'd given her housekeeper the weekend off so nobody found her until the Monday morning, in fact.'

'Where was Freddie when it happened?'

'In the house with her.' Jack's expression was grim. 'The police think that India died on the Saturday afternoon, so Freddie was there on his own until the housekeeper returned.' His voice caught and she could tell how hard he found it to rein in his emotions. 'When they found India, she was surrounded by bits of biscuit and pieces of fruit. They think that Freddie had been trying to feed her.'

'Oh, how awful!' Alison's eyes filled with tears as she pictured the scene. 'The poor little mite must have been terrified.'

'He still is. He hasn't said a word since it happened. Apparently, he used to chat away before, but he's totally withdrawn into his own little world now.' Jack kissed the top of the child's head. 'I've tried everything I can think of to get through to him but nothing seems to work. It's no wonder when you think what he's been through. His whole world has been torn apart. Despite India's faults, she genuinely loved him, and it's going to be hard to make up for the loss he's suffered.'

'I wish I could think of something to make it easier for

you—for you and Freddie, I mean,' she added hurriedly, before he got the wrong idea. It was concern for the child which had moved her most, she told herself firmly. Jack was capable of looking after himself, surely?

The doubt crept in on the coattails of her determination to be sensible and she cleared her throat. 'How is he now? Does he seem any better?'

'A bit. He's definitely not as feverish as he was, but I think I'll get him checked out at the surgery tomorrow just to make sure.'

'Really?' Alison's brows rose. 'You don't trust your own judgement?'

'Nope. Not when it comes to Freddie, anyway.' He smiled at her, a lazily seductive curl of his lips that did horrendous things to her blood pressure. 'I'd prefer him to see someone who knows a bit more about paediatrics. I couldn't find any sign of a rash or anything like that when I examined him, but I'm no expert when it comes to childhood ailments. I would hate to have missed something vital.'

Alison was surprised by his honesty and said so. 'Not many doctors would admit that.'

'No?' He shrugged, his broad shoulders moving lightly under the battered old leather jacket he was wearing. 'I can't see the point of boosting my ego at Freddie's expense. I know my own strengths and my weaknesses. Put me in an operating theatre and I'll give it everything I've got, but I'm nowhere near as confident when it comes to measles and mumps!'

'That's one way of looking at it.' Alison laughed.

Jack laughed as well. 'It's the only way I know,' he agreed, smiling at her.

Alison looked away when she felt her heart flutter. Maybe Jack did seem to appreciate her help, but it would be foolish to get too carried away by the idea. In the glamorous, high-society world in which he moved, she wouldn't register as the tiniest blip on the social scale.

'I'd better go.' Jack announced. He wrapped Freddie up in the blanket and stood up. 'I've taken up far too much of your time as it is. Thanks for all your help tonight, Alison. I really appreciate it.'

'It was nothing.' Alison followed him to the door. 'I know what it's like when you have sick child to worry about.'

'Lucy mentioned something about you having a little boy?'

'That's right. Sam's three—the same age as Freddie, in fact.'

Jack paused beside the front door. 'How do you manage when you're working? Does your little chap go to a nursery?'

'He goes to nursery every morning, then to a childminder in the afternoon.'

Jack frowned. 'Do you think that's a better system than leaving him in nursery all day?'

'Not really. I can't afford the nursery fees for a full day's care. This way is cheaper.'

'Oh, I see. Right.'

He sounded embarrassed and Alison hurried to reassure him, wondering why it mattered how he felt. It wasn't as though she and Jack were going to become close friends. She didn't move in his circle and he most certainly wouldn't be interested in moving in hers.

The thought was dispiriting and she chased it away. 'I'm happy with the arrangement. Sam loves Carol, the childminder. She also looks after a couple of the other children from the nursery in the afternoons and he has lots of fun when he's with her.'

'It sounds great. I might consider that kind of arrangement myself once I get sorted out.' He grimaced. 'I'm afraid

I took the easy option and booked Freddie into the nursery full time, although I'm not convinced it's the best thing for him at the moment.'

'You can't look after him and go to work,' she pointed out, and he sighed.

'I suppose so. It's the old rock and hard place scenario, isn't it? I want to be there for him, but I also need to provide for him. Being a parent isn't easy.'

'It isn't, but the rewards are huge,' she assured him.

'I know. Even though Freddie only tolerates me, I can't imagine being without him now.'

He gave her a quick smile, then opened the door. Alison followed him out to the step, shivering as a blast of cold air roared across from the bay. Jack turned to her.

'Thanks again, Alison. You've been great.'

He leant forward and kissed her lightly on her cheek, then strode off down the road. Alison went back inside, her hands shaking as she closed the door. She went back to the sitting room and loaded the cups onto the tray, then carried it into the kitchen, and all the time she was doing so her heart was bouncing up and down like a yo-yo on a string.

Heat flowed through her as she recalled the feel of Jack's lips on her skin. The kiss must have lasted no longer than a second yet she knew it would be imprinted in her memory for an awful lot longer. It wasn't just the fact that it had been a long time since a man had kissed her either—she could have dealt with that. It was the fact that it was Jack who had kissed her, *Jack's* lips which had left this imprint on her cheek.

Lifting her hand to her face, she touched the spot and shuddered. It was going to take a long time before the memory faded.

CHAPTER THREE

SATURDAY dawned bright and clear. When Jack opened the front door, he detected a definite hint of spring in the air. Scooping Freddie into his arms, he carried him to the car and strapped him in. Although the child seemed a lot better that morning, he still intended to have him checked over. As he'd told Alison last night, he wasn't taking any chances with his son's health.

Jack frowned as he slid behind the wheel. It was strange how he had found himself opening up to Alison. Normally, he shied away from discussing his private life with anyone else, yet he'd had no hesitation about telling her all about India and Freddie. Was it the fact that she had the rare ability to combine practicality with sympathy that had made him reveal so much? he wondered as he started the engine. True, there'd been a couple of occasions when he had first arrived at her house when she'd seemed a little prickly, but he had put that down to the fact that she hadn't had time to get to know him then. However, it appeared that his initial assessment, that she had taken a dislike to him, might have been wide of the mark, and he found that an incredibly comforting thought. For some reason he couldn't explain, he wanted Alison on his side.

There was just one other car parked in the surgery's car park when he arrived. Saturday morning surgery was for urgent cases only and the townsfolk understood that. Although most general practices had cancelled Saturday surgeries, Jack knew that his father had decided against such a step. Nick Tremayne preferred a more traditional approach, so the doctors working at Penhally Bay Surgery did their own night calls as well. While Jack admired his father's dedication, he also resented it. He had never been able to rid himself of the thought that if Nick had been less committed to his job, he might have had more time for his own family.

Jack lifted Freddie out of his seat and carried him inside. Hazel Furse, the surgery's newly appointed practice manager, smiled broadly when he went in.

'Jack! How lovely to see you.'

'Hi, Hazel, how are you doing?' Jack replied, walking over to the desk. 'I believe congratulations are in order following your promotion.'

'Thank you. I was thrilled to be offered the job when Kate left.' Hazel smiled at Freddie. 'Is this your little boy?'

'Yes, this is Freddie. He's been running a bit of a temperature and I wondered if someone would have a look at him for me. Who's on duty this morning?'

'Your father,' Hazel replied cheerfully. Reaching into a drawer, she took out a new patient form, mercifully missing Jack's grimace. He'd been hoping to avoid his father until he was settled in, but obviously it wasn't to be.

'You can drop this in any time you like,' Hazel explained, handing him the form. 'You're in luck because we're really quiet this morning, so you can go straight in. It's such a lovely day that nobody wants to waste it by seeing the doctor.'

'Great. Thanks.'

Jack tried to summon up some enthusiasm as he knocked on the consulting-room door. He went in when Nick bade him enter, forcing himself to smile when his father looked up. 'Morning, Dad. I thought I'd bring Freddie in for a check-up. He was running a temperature last night and although I couldn't find anything obviously wrong with him, I wanted to make sure there was nothing nasty brewing.'

'Bring him over here.'

Nick's expression was difficult to read as he got up and walked around the desk. Jack couldn't tell if his father was pleased to see him or totally indifferent as he made his way to the couch. He placed his son on the bed and stood beside him. 'There's no need to be scared, Freddie,' he said softly, when the little boy began to whimper.

'Hello, Freddie.' Nick bent down and smiled at the child. 'I'm just going to feel your tummy and then listen to your chest. Do you think you can do me a really big favour and hold this for me?'

Nick offered the child his stethoscope, and to Jack's amazement Freddie accepted it. He shook his head as he watched his son clutching it in his chubby little hands.

'He's usually terrified of strangers. I've never known him accept anything before.'

'I'm not exactly a stranger, though, am I?' Nick said flatly, bending over the child.

Jack bit back his sharp retort. This was neither the time nor the place to start one of their infamous arguments. He watched as his father examined Freddie, reluctantly admiring the fact that Nick was able to perform the task without causing the child any distress. He mentally ticked off the procedures as his father performed them: a visual examination of Freddie's ears, eyes, nose and throat; a careful inspection of his skin to check for a rash; palpating his abdomen; and feeling his armpits for any signs of tenderness or swelling.

'Has he had a cold recently?' Nick asked, glancing up.

'No, nothing at all. Physically, he's been quite well.'

Nick's gaze sharpened. 'How is he mentally? Lucy said that he has stopped talking—is that right?'

'Yes. That's why it was so difficult to work out what was wrong with him last night—he wouldn't tell me.' Jack sighed. 'I've tried everything I can think of to encourage him to speak, but he still won't talk to me or anyone else.'

'He needs time to get over the trauma,' Nick said bluntly. 'It's not going to happen overnight and you need to be patient.'

He turned and smiled at the little boy, not giving Jack a chance to explain that he already knew that. 'Can I have that back now, Freddie? Thank you. That's a good boy.'

Jack gritted his teeth while Nick listened to Freddie's chest. He wasn't going to snap back, and certainly wasn't going to appear as though he was on the defensive. 'So what do you think?' he asked mildly after his father had finished.

'I'd say it was his teeth. The second molar on the right of his lower jaw has recently erupted, and I'd lay good money on that being what has been causing the problem. A lot of children feel very out of sorts when they're teething.'

'A new tooth? I never thought of that!' Jack exclaimed, feeling incredibly foolish for having overlooked something so simple.

Nick shrugged. 'It's an easy mistake to make. After all, Freddie is three and you probably assumed he was past the teething stage by now.'

'I did.'

Jack grimaced as he lifted his son down from the couch. Although he was relieved that Freddie wasn't sickening for something serious, it was galling to wonder if his father now believed he was incompetent.

He pushed the thought aside, because he wasn't going

down that route again. He had spent far too much of his life trying to gain Nick's approval, and he had made up his mind a long time ago that he wasn't going to carry on beating his head against the proverbial brick wall. Nick could think whatever he liked. *He* knew that he was a damned good surgeon and he didn't need anyone's approbation to prove that to him.

'Well, thanks for that,' Jack said stiffly, taking hold of Freddie's hand.

'It's what I'm here for.' Nick sat down behind his desk. 'Just keep giving him junior paracetamol and it should settle down in a day or so.'

'Right. Thanks. I will.' Jack headed for the door, then paused when his father carried on.

'Have you seen Lucy yet?'

'Yes, she called round late yesterday afternoon after she'd finished here.'

'Good. It will be a big help to you, having Lucy on hand,' Nick said quietly.

Jack felt a shaft of pain run through him. Had that been a subtle hint that Nick himself wasn't going to offer a helping hand if he needed it? His expression hardened as he opened the door. 'It will. At least there's one member of my family who's willing to help out.'

'That wasn't what I meant,' Nick began, but Jack didn't wait to hear what he had to say. He wasn't interested.

He shook his head as he stepped out into the corridor. There was no point wishing that his father gave a damn about him *or* his son. He knew what Nick thought of him because he had made it perfectly clear that he disliked the way Jack had chosen to live his life. OK, so maybe he *had* gone a bit wild a few years ago—he was willing to admit that. He had spent a lot of time on the London party scene, although in his own defence he had never let it interfere with his work. However, in the past couple of years—ever since his mother had died—he had cut out the socialising and concentrated on his career.

He was no longer the playboy Nick imagined him to be, although his father would never accept that. Nick seemed to prefer to think the worst of him, and if that was how he felt then Jack wasn't going to try to change his mind. As for him and Freddie, they would manage perfectly well without Nick's help. He had Lucy to help him if he got really stuck, and if she was busy he would sort things out himself. Just for a moment his mind flashed back to the empathy he'd seen in Alison's eyes the previous night before he blanked out the memory. Alison had enough to contend with without taking on his problems as well.

Nick got up after the door closed and went to the window. He sighed as he watched Jack lift little Freddie into the car. He should have gone after him and made him listen, instead of letting him rush off like that. Now Jack believed that he wasn't interested in his grandson, and that couldn't be further from the truth.

Of course he cared about the little boy, just as he cared about Jack, too. The trouble was that every time he and Jack were together they ended up arguing. Annabel had said it was because he and Jack were so alike—they were both strong-minded and passionate about issues they cared deeply about.

Maybe it was true, but it didn't help to resolve this issue. Jack needed his help more than ever at the moment, and he wanted to be there for him and Freddie. It was how to convince Jack of that fact which was going to be the hardest thing to do.

Alison was on her way back to Penhally Bay when the accident happened. She'd been to the local farmers' market to buy some fresh fruit and veg. Sam had been invited to a birthday party at his childminder's home so she had taken advantage of the fact that she'd had a couple of hours to herself. She was driving back along the narrow winding lanes when a car overtook her, travelling far too fast. It reached the bend and she saw its brake lights flash on as the driver tried to slow down, but it was too late by then. It careered across the road and she gasped in horror when she saw a tractor suddenly appear, travelling in the opposite direction. There was a sickening crunch of metal as the two vehicles collided.

Alison braked to a stop and reached for her mobile phone to call the emergency services. Once she was sure the ambulances were on their way, she jumped out of her car and ran over to the vehicles. The car had rolled over onto its roof; its windows were shattered and most of its bodywork had been stoved in by the force of the impact. The tractor had fared rather better—it was still upright but the driver looked dazed as he staggered down from the cab.

'There was nothing I could do,' he said when Alison hurried over to him. 'I tried to stop but it all happened so fast…'

He swayed and she grabbed hold of his arm and led him to the grass verge. 'Sit down there,' she instructed, crouching in front of him. 'Did you hurt yourself?'

'I think I must have hit my head,' he said vaguely, touching the side of his head.

Alison gently explored the area, sucking in her breath when she felt a definite depression in the skull above his right ear. 'You've had quite a bump,' she said, trying to hide her alarm. An injury like this could cause untold problems if it wasn't attended to promptly.

'Aye. It feels like it, too,' the man replied gruffly. He

suddenly started to shiver, as reaction set in, so she took off her coat and wrapped it around him.

'I'm going to have a look at the people in the car,' she explained. 'Just stay there until I come back.'

He nodded, and she frowned when she realised that he was definitely less responsive than he had been initially. She propped him against the wall, desperately wishing there was something more she could do for him. However, it would need more than first aid to sort out his injuries.

She ran over to the car and knelt down so she could peer through the rear window. The driver was dangling upside down from his seat belt. He was cursing loudly and didn't appear to be badly injured, from what she could see. She left him there and went to check on the passenger, a teenage girl who hadn't fared nearly as well. She obviously hadn't been wearing a seat belt because she had gone straight through the windscreen when the car had overturned. Alison found her lying in the road and could barely conceal her horror when she saw the injuries to the girl's face. She was conscious, though, and responded when Alison asked her name.

'Becca.' She raised a trembling hand to her face but Alison stopped her.

'No, you mustn't touch your face, my love. We need to make sure that it stays as clean as possible.'

'It hurts,' Becca whimpered.

'I know it does, but the ambulance will be here soon and the doctors will sort it all out at the hospital for you,' she explained, mentally crossing her fingers. From what she could see, the damage was so extensive that it would need major surgery to put everything back together, although she had no intention of telling the poor girl that.

She stood up and smiled at her. 'I'm going to fetch some dressings from my car. We need to keep the germs out of those cuts.'

'Are you a doctor?' Becca whispered.

'No, I'm a nurse,' Alison explained. She patted Becca's arm. 'I'll only be a moment—stay there and don't worry.'

She left Becca sitting on the ground and checked on the driver again. He had managed to unfasten his seat belt and had crawled out through the rear window. He was holding his head in his hands when Alison reached him.

'How are you?' she asked, crouching down.

'How do you think?' He rubbed his hands over his face and groaned. 'I'm going to have a king-sized headache in the morning!'

Alison frowned. She couldn't be sure, but she thought she could smell alcohol on his breath. 'Have you been drinking?'

'Why? What's it got to do with you?' he shot back, glaring at her.

She stood up, having neither the time nor the patience to argue with him. 'Not a lot, but I'm sure the police will be interested if you have.'

He swore loudly, but she ignored him as she went to check on the tractor driver again. He was unconscious now, so she placed him in the recovery position, frowning when she heard how noisy his breathing was. His face was very flushed as well, and when she checked his pulse, it was heavy and bounding but extremely slow. He was exhibiting all the signs of compression, in fact, so Alison took out her phone and called Ambulance Control so they could alert the hospital. If blood was collecting inside the man's skull and putting pressure on his brain, it would need to be drained away as soon as possible.

Although she hated leaving him on his own, she had to go back to Becca. She found some lint-free, sterile cloths in her case and took them with her. She snipped holes for the girl's eyes, nose and mouth, then gently covered her face to minimise the risk of infection getting into the tissue, but didn't do anything else in case she caused more damage. Becca was trembling with shock after Alison finished, and she put her arm around her.

'It won't be long now, sweetheart. The ambulance is on its way.'

'Is Toby all right?' Becca whispered through the dressings.

'If Toby is the driver of the car, he's fine.'

Becca hesitated for a moment before the words came rushing out. 'He'd been drinking last night. I had no idea until we set off or I would never have got in the car with him. I was really scared, because he kept weaving in and out of the traffic when we were on the motorway. And when we got into the country he just put his foot down. When we came to a junction, I took off my seat belt and begged him to let me out of the car, but he just laughed and drove even faster.'

Alison sighed. 'He did a very reckless and stupid thing. Alcohol stays in the body for hours, and nobody who's been drinking heavily at night should get in a car and drive the following morning.'

'I know that,' Becca said miserably. 'But Toby never listens to what anyone says.'

'What were you doing here in the first place? You're obviously not local.'

'No, we're from London. We're boarders at the same school. Toby's parents have a holiday home in Rock and he invited everyone down there tonight for a party. I was going to travel on the coach with some of our friends but Toby said he would give me a lift.' Tears welled to her eyes. 'My mum and dad are away and they have no idea that I got a weekend pass from school. They'll go mad when they find out what's happened!'

'Don't worry about that now,' Alison said softly.

There wasn't time to say anything else because the ambulances arrived just then, quickly followed by the police. Alison handed Becca over to the paramedics and went back to the tractor driver, even though there was very little she could do for him. She gave the paramedics a full report, then the police took a statement from her and she was free to leave. However, she couldn't help thinking about what Becca had told her. She couldn't bear to think of the poor girl being on her own until her parents arrived.

She got back into her car and followed the ambulances to St Piran Hospital. She found a parking space, then hurried through to the A and E department. It was extremely busy, and she had to wait her turn before she could explain to the receptionist why she was there.

By the time she got through to the treatment area Becca had been seen by the duty doctor. He took Alison aside and explained that the girl needed specialist care for her injuries and that they were waiting for one of the surgeons to see her. Alison went into the cubicle and sat with her, doing her best to keep Becca calm while they waited for the surgeon to arrive. It seemed to take for ever before the curtain swished back, and she gasped when Jack appeared.

'What are you doing here?'

'They had a rush on—a major pile-up just outside Boscastle—so I got called in,' he explained, with a smile that immediately set her heart off on its yo-yo tactics again. 'What's your excuse?'

'I happened to be driving along the road when this accident happened,' Alison replied primly, in case he thought she had dreamt up an excuse to see him. 'I stopped and helped.'

'Thank heavens you did. At least you knew what to do

and didn't make my job more difficult by trying to patch things up,' he said warmly as he walked over to the bed.

Alison felt a little glow erupt inside her at the praise. She moved aside, not wanting to crowd him while he examined his patient. He smiled at the girl as he sat down on the edge of the bed.

'Hi, it's Rebecca, isn't it?'

'Everyone calls me Becca,' she shyly corrected him.

'Hmm, pretty name. It suits you. I'm Jack Tremayne, one of the surgical staff here. Now, let's take a look and see what's happened to you.'

He pulled on a fresh pair of gloves, then examined the girl's injuries, taking his time as he studied every part of her face. Peeling off the gloves, he rolled them into a ball and tossed them into the bin.

'Right, Becca, I'm not going to lie to you. You have some really nasty cuts there. There's bits of gravel and other muck in them, too, and that will need to be cleaned away before I do anything else, otherwise the dirt will be tattooed into your skin—and we don't want that happening, do we?'

'No.' Tears began to leak from Becca's eyes again. 'Am I going to look like a freak?'

'No way!' Jack grinned as he held out his hands and waggled them under her nose. 'These hands don't know how to do freaky. I give you my word that I'll have you looking almost as good as new, but it will take time. There isn't going to be a quick fix, sweetheart. It's going to take time and patience, but we have loads of both to spare, don't we?'

'I guess so,' Becca agreed, obviously reassured by his upbeat manner.

Alison smiled when she heard how much more positive the girl sounded. Jack had struck exactly the right note—not too formal, not too scary, but truthful, too—and she was impressed. Mind you, she was impressed by a lot of things he did. She hurriedly cleared her mind of such nonsense as he continued.

'The worst injury is to your left cheek. A flap of skin has been pulled away and that will need to be reattached. Hopefully, the blood supply can be restored, but it might need a skin graft as well as some fancy needlework to put it back together.'

'You mean that you will have to take bits of skin from somewhere else?' Becca said, sounding a little unsure about the idea.

'Yes, although it sounds far worse than it is. Basically, what it means is that I will find an area where the skin tone matches the colour of your face—behind the ear is usually the best place. I'll remove just enough skin to cover the injury and transplant it to your cheek. Hey presto—problem solved.' He patted Becca's hand. 'It's not certain that it will have to happen yet, so we'll worry about it if and when, shall we?'

He stood up when Becca nodded. 'Right. I'm going to take you to Theatre and make a start. I believe your parents are away and that your aunt and uncle are trying to contact them?'

'Yes. Mum will go mad when she sees the state of me…'

Jack leant over and squeezed her hand. 'No, she won't. She'll just be so glad that you're all right that she won't think about anything else.'

'Do you honestly think so?' Becca said wistfully. 'Is that what your mum would do?'

An expression of pain crossed Jack's face before he turned away. 'Yep. That's exactly what my mum would do, so trust me, Becca. You have nothing to worry about on that score.'

Alison's heart went out to him. Everyone in Penhally Bay had been shocked and saddened when Jack's mother, Annabel Tremayne, had died, so how much worse must it be for Jack? She followed him out of the cubicle, wanting in some way to make him feel better about the loss he had suffered.

'Are you all right?'

'Yes. It still gets to me at times, though.' He gave her a sad smile. 'Daft, isn't it? It's two years since Mum died and I should have come to terms with it by now.'

'Not at all. It's only natural that you should miss Annabel. She was your mother and you loved her—it's understandable that you should feel sad because she isn't here any longer.'

'I think the hardest thing is knowing that Freddie will never meet her. Mum would have been thrilled about having a grandson as well as a granddaughter.'

'At least Freddie will be able to get to know his granddad,' Alison pointed out.

'Hmm. If his granddad is interested in getting to know *him*.'

Alison looked at him in astonishment. 'But Nick was over the moon when he found out about Freddie. He told everyone about him.'

'Really?'

Jack didn't attempt to hide his scepticism and she laughed. 'Yes, really. I doubt there's anyone left in Penhally Bay who doesn't know about the doctor's little grandson.'

Jack shook his head in amazement. 'I'd never have believed it, to be honest. I thought Dad would have kept it very quiet. I mean, the fact that your son has found out he has a child he knew nothing about isn't really something to brag about.'

'That may be your take on the situation but it's definitely not Nick's,' Alison said firmly. She glanced round when she heard someone coming along the corridor. 'Anyway, I'd better not keep you. Good luck with the op. I hope everything goes smoothly.'

'Thanks.' Jack started to walk away, then suddenly turned back. 'And thanks for what you told me just now about my dad. It meant a lot to me, Alison. Really it did.'

He gave her a quick smile and left, but Alison was in no doubt that he'd meant what he'd said. There was a warm feeling inside her as she went back into the cubicle, a sense of satisfaction that in some small way she had made Jack happy.

She sighed. She could get addicted to the feeling if she weren't careful and, like any addiction, it could prove to be extremely dangerous.

CHAPTER FOUR

'ANGIE, Dave, Mel, Parkash… Oh, and that's Lilian in the corner.'

'Hi, nice to meet you all.'

Jack nodded hello to his new workmates as he approached the table. Becca had been prepped and was fully anaesthetised now. Although Jack could have done some of the work under local anaesthetic—some of the scrubbing and debriding—he'd decided it would be less stressful for the girl if she wasn't aware of what was happening.

'You're quite happy about this, Jack? I know it was an imposition to drag you in here today…'

'But you had no choice.'

Jack smiled at his new boss. Although he had met Alexandra Ross only briefly at his interview, he had taken an immediate liking to her. In her late thirties, Alex had a reputation for being a first-rate surgeon, and Jack felt privileged to be working with her. She had been head of surgery at one of the major London teaching hospitals before she had moved to Cornwall the previous year. Jack wasn't sure why she had made the move but he was glad that she had. It was good to know that he had someone of her calibre to supervise him while he finished his training.

'I was glad to help, Alex, so don't give it another thought.

My contract started on Friday anyway, so it's not as though I'm breaking any rules by being here.'

'Definitely not, although I have to admit that breaking rules wasn't my first concern.' Alex returned his smile. 'I hope you managed to sort out some child care without too much hassle?'

'It wasn't a problem,' Jack assured her, trying not to think about how Freddie had cried when he had left him with Lucy. He had to forget about his personal problems and concentrate on the task ahead.

Pulling the mask over his nose and mouth, he bent over the table. As he'd told Becca, his first job was to remove all the muck from the various cuts and then see what he was left with. It wasn't a job he could rush, and he didn't intend to do so either. Becca's future happiness was in his hands, and he was very aware of that fact as he set to work.

Using a tiny metal scrubber, he carefully cleaned away all the grit. He was so absorbed that he merely nodded when Alex told him that she would leave him to get on with it. Although it was a compliment to his skills not to be supervised at every step, he wouldn't have expected anything less. He was good at his job, and the people he worked with soon realised that.

'Can I have some more saline over here?' he asked, glancing at the circulating nurse. He nodded when she washed away the minute particles of grime that he had removed from a cut on Becca's forehead. 'Thanks.'

'You're welcome.'

Jack saw her eyes crinkle above her mask and smiled back. He believed in fostering a good working relationship with the other members of the team and was pleased that they seemed so willing to accept him. 'I hope you still feel like that in a couple of hours' time,' he joked, and everyone laughed.

'Don't worry, Mel will soon let you know if you're in her bad books,' the anaesthetist, Parkash Patel, informed him. 'Take it from me, Mel has her own highly effective way of making her displeasure felt!'

'That sounds ominous. I must try really hard not upset her.' Jack chuckled when Mel grunted loudly to indicate her displeasure at being so unjustly criticised. 'Whoops! Looks like I've just earned my first black mark.'

He bent over the table again, feeling himself relax as he carried on. Surgery was the only thing he had ever wanted to do. However, when he had discovered the difference he could make to people's lives through plastic surgery, he'd known he had found his true calling.

Plastic surgery improved both the function and the appearance of a patient's body. Although some surgeons were sniffy about the value of cosmetic plastic surgery, Jack believed in that too, especially when it was used to rectify the devastating effects caused by an illness or an accident. His long-term goal was to have his own clinic, where he could help people regain their lives by restoring their looks as well as the functionality of their bodies. It was very much in the future at the moment, but it was what he was aiming for.

Fired up by his belief in what he was doing, Jack lost himself in his work. Once he was sure all the dirt had been removed he began the delicate task of stitching the cuts. Lilian, the SHO, watched entranced as he used the tiniest stitches to bring the skin together.

'I don't know how you know where it all fits!' she exclaimed. 'It looks such a mess that I wouldn't know the best place to start.'

'It's really quite simple,' Jack said, easing a tiny flap of torn skin back into its rightful place. 'You find the places where the skin seems to fit the most easily and join them together first. After that, the rest should fall into place. The one thing you must be careful about, though, is that you don't cut away too much tissue when you are debriding an area or you'll never be able to match things up.'

'Why are you using interrupted sutures? Continuous ones would be a lot quicker.'

'Yes, but they don't give as good a result. It's not speed but the quality of your work that will determine the outcome for this patient for the rest of her life. Cut conservatively, match with care and use the smallest stitches, and there's a very good chance she will thank you for it in later life and not blame you.'

'I don't think my suturing will ever be that neat,' Lilian said wistfully, and Jack laughed.

'Then practise! It's like everything else—you need to do as much as you can before you get the hang of it.'

It took another two hours before he was satisfied that he had done all he could for now. The large tear on Becca's left cheek was the thing that worried him most. There'd been too much tissue damage to match the edges successfully. It would need a skin graft, and that was something he'd have to do at a later date. He sighed as he straightened up.

'That's about all we can do for now. Thanks for all your help. It's been really great working with you.' He moved away from the table, then stopped when he heard everyone applauding. Glancing back, he shook his head. 'What's that for?'

'Well, we definitely don't want you getting too big for your boots,' Mel informed him tartly, 'but I think we all agree that was an excellent performance, don't we, folks?'

Jack chuckled when everyone chorused their agreement. 'I don't know what to say, guys.'

'How about "the drinks are on me"?' Dave, the theatre orderly, chirped up.

Jack grimaced. 'Nothing would give me greater pleasure,

but I'll have to take a rain-check for now. I've left my sister babysitting my little boy and I need to get back before chaos breaks out. Can we make it next week? I promise I'll get myself organised by then,' he said, crossing his fingers behind his back.

He left Theatre and headed to the changing room, wondering if he would be able to keep his promise. He was loath to leave Freddie, apart from when he had to go to work, and he wasn't sure if it would be right to take an hour or so off to get to know his new colleagues better.

He sighed as he stepped into the shower. Adapting to life as a single father took some getting used to, but he would manage. He had to. He definitely wasn't going to let Freddie down, no matter what sacrifices he had to make. If he had no social life, so what? He'd done more than his share of partying and he was happy to leave all that behind him now. Basically, there was nothing he needed apart from Freddie and his work.

Scooping a handful of soap out of the dispenser, Jack lathered his chest, then paused. There was one issue he hadn't considered—mainly because it had never been an issue before. He had never had a serious relationship with a woman. Even his relationship with India had been a casual affair. But what if he met someone and fell in love with her—how would he juggle that with being a dad? If it was hard to get away for a quick drink with his colleagues, how would he find the time to spend with her? And, on the flip side, how would *she* feel about the fact that he had a ready-made family?

Jack frowned as he rinsed off the lather. He couldn't answer any of those questions. It was a case of having to wait and see what happened. He wasn't even sure what had put the idea into his head in the first place. After all, it wasn't as though he had spent much time thinking about the woman he would eventually marry. He'd been far too busy working and enjoying himself. But now he found himself giving it serious thought.

What would she be like, this woman who pressed all the right buttons? He had always fancied sultry, elegant brunettes in the past, but for some reason he found it difficult to summon up a picture of his ideal woman. Perhaps he should start with her character rather than her looks, he decided. He wanted someone who was intelligent and kind, someone who would share his interests but have interests of her own as well. He definitely didn't want a woman who hung onto his every word—that would be too boring!

He grabbed a towel off the rack, wrapped it around his waist and stepped out of the cubicle. So he wanted a woman with a mind of her own, who was independent enough to have her own opinions and yet not be at odds with him over really important issues. She would have to be understanding, too, because his job was so demanding that it took up a lot of his time and he would hate it if it caused friction between them. She would also have to like children, and he would need to be sure that she would accept Freddie as her own.

That just about summed up her personality so maybe he would have better luck with the matter of her appearance?

Jack tossed the wet towel into the hamper and started to get dressed. Underwear, jeans, T-shirt… He paused. A picture was forming in his mind's eye and he frowned as he tried to bring it into focus—soft fair hair, hazel eyes, a curvy figure… He gasped when he realised it was Alison Myers he was picturing. Why on earth had he conjured *her* up as his ideal woman? Because she was pretty and kind, and ticked all the other boxes on his list?

He dragged a T-shirt over his head and grabbed his jacket. He must be in a worse state than he'd realised if he was dredging up such rubbish. There was no chance of him and Alison becoming an item. No chance at all.

Monday morning rolled around and Alison found herself rushing to get ready. Mornings were always hectic, what with Sam needing to be taken to nursery and her having to get to work on time. As soon as Sam had finished his breakfast, she popped on his coat and walked him to the nursery. There were a lot of parents there, most of them in cars, too, and she kept tight hold of Sam's hand as they crossed the road. She had just reached the pavement when a car pulled up beside her and Jack got out.

'Hi. It's chaos, isn't it? Is it always like this?' he asked, opening the rear door.

'Mornings are usually very busy,' Alison agreed as she paused. She cleared her throat when she heard how husky her voice sounded, but the sight of Jack bundled up in a navy ski jacket with his dark hair all mussed seemed to have stolen her breath. 'What time did you get back from the hospital on Saturday?' she said, striving for normality.

'Just after seven.' He lifted Freddie out of the car and smiled at her. 'How about you?'

'Oh, I was back home by four.' She started walking towards the nursery gates, unsure whether she should wait for Jack, but he solved the problem by catching up with her.

'At least it wasn't too late.' He glanced at the other parents and grimaced. 'What's the routine? Do you take the kids straight into their classrooms?'

'Yes. They have to be signed in first, though, so that the staff know they're here.' Alison led the way through the main door then glanced back. 'Has Freddie been to nursery before?'

'Yes. He was enrolled at a nursery school in London, so I'm hoping that will help him settle down here. If he gets back into some sort of familiar routine, it might make him feel more secure.'

'Don't be surprised if he's upset when it's time for you to leave him,' Alison warned him. 'Sam used to be really clingy—although he soon got over it,' she added when she saw the worry on Jack's face.

'Freddie isn't so much clingy as terrified.' Jack sighed as he ran his hand over his son's dark curls. 'I don't think he cares one way or the other if I'm around, to be honest, but he's scared of being left in strange places.'

'Have you spoken to the staff about his problems?' Alison asked quietly so none of the other parents could overhear.

'Yes. I've had several long conversations with Mrs Galloway, who owns the nursery. She promised to alert the staff to the problem and I'm hoping she's done so.'

'Christine won't have forgotten,' Alison assured him. 'She's completely devoted to the children. That's why this school has such a wonderful reputation—and why there's a waiting list for places, too.'

'Really?' Jack frowned. 'I hadn't realised that. I mean, I had no problems about getting Freddie a place here.'

'I think your father had a word with Christine,' Alison explained, then wondered if she should have mentioned it when Jack frowned.

There was no time to say anything else. They had reached the head of the queue and she busied herself signing Sam in. She took him to the cloakroom and helped him hang his coat on his hook—the one with the bright green frog on it—then took him into the playroom.

'I'll see you at lunchtime, sweetheart,' she said, giving him a hug.

'Bye, Mummy,' he replied dutifully, before he raced away to join his friends. Alison smiled as she headed to the door. There was no sign of clinginess now, thank heavens!

Jack was talking to Trish Atkins, who was in charge of the three-year-olds, and Alison didn't interrupt them. She simply waved as she passed and hurried out of the door. Glancing at her watch, she realised that she would have to get a move on if she wasn't going to be late for her first appointment.

She made it to the surgery with five minutes to spare. Sue was on duty at the reception desk that morning, and she grinned when Alison rushed in.

'You look as though you've run the three-minute mile.'

'It feels like it, too,' Alison gasped. She glanced around the waiting room and discovered that her first patient had beaten her to it. 'Just give me a minute to take off my coat, then you can send Mrs Baxter up. Oh, and tell her to use the lift, would you? I don't want her climbing the stairs.'

Alison hurried up the stairs, turning right when she reached the top. The nurse's room was at the end of the corridor, next to the lift, and she left the door open so she could hear her patient arrive. She hung her coat on a peg, then booted up her computer and brought up Audrey Baxter's notes.

Mrs Baxter had been diagnosed recently with angina, a condition whereby insufficient oxygen was carried via the blood to the heart. Although there were a number of causes for the condition, the most usual one was atherosclerosis—a build-up of fatty deposits within the arteries which caused them to narrow. Dr Donnelly had requested a cholesterol test, which was why Audrey had an appointment with her that morning.

Alison got up and popped her head round the door when she heard the lift arrive. 'This way, Mrs Baxter. Come straight through.'

'Right you are, my lovely,' Audrey Baxter replied cheerfully. In her early sixties, Audrey had worked at the post office until she had retired the previous year. She now helped out at the church, and was always cheerful and always abreast of all the local gossip. She smiled as she plonked herself down onto a chair.

'I was glad to take the lift, I can tell you. I've been feeling a bit breathless this morning.'

'Are you having pains in your chest?' Alison asked in concern.

'Not really pains, as such. It just feels a bit tight, as though something's pressing on it.'

'I'll give Dr Donnelly a call and ask him to take a look at you,' Alison said immediately. She dialled Adam's extension but there was no reply, so she phoned the reception desk. 'Has Adam arrived yet?'

'No. He just phoned to say that he'll be late because he had an early callout,' Sue explained. 'Nick's here, if you need him.'

'Thanks, Sue. I'll give him a call.'

Alison phoned Nick's extension and explained that she would like him to see a patient. He arrived a few minutes later and she quickly explained the situation before he examined Audrey.

'Have you been taking the low-dose aspirin that Dr Donnelly prescribed for you?' Nick asked after he'd finished listening to Audrey's heart.

'Well, no, not really.' Audrey looked sheepish. 'It seemed a bit daft to take tablets when I was feeling fine, so I've only been taking them whenever I have a pain in my chest.'

'I see. How about the glycerol trinitrate spray? I assume that Dr Donnelly advised you to use it if you had any pains or constriction in your chest?'

'Um…well, yes, he did,' Audrey admitted.

Nick shook his head. 'You need to follow Dr Donnelly's advice. If you don't, the situation will only deteriorate.

Aspirin thins the blood and helps avoid the danger of clots forming, but it won't work if the tablets are left in the packet. And you must carry your spray with you wherever you go, in case you need it.'

'I shall, Dr Tremayne,' Audrey promised, looking suitably repentant.

'Make sure you do,' Nick said firmly. 'You're not helping yourself by not taking the medication. You could, in fact, be putting yourself at greater risk of having a heart attack.' He waited to see if that had sunk in then nodded to Alison. 'I'll leave you to get on with the blood test. Call me if you need me again.'

'Thank you.'

Alison picked up the dish containing the syringe and plastic vials and took it over to her desk. She smiled at Audrey. 'I hope you've taken heed of all that.'

'Oh, I have.' Audrey raised an eyebrow. 'He can be a bit stern, can Dr Tremayne, when he chooses, can't he?'

'Only because he has your best interests at heart,' she assured her. She took the samples and sealed them into a plastic envelope bearing both the patient's and the surgery's details. 'We should have the results back by the end of the week, so make an appointment to see Dr Donnelly on your way out.'

Alison cleared everything away, then buzzed for her next patient. However, as she waited for him to arrive she found herself comparing Nick's approach to that of his son. Jack had exhibited none of the brusqueness that Nick occasionally showed towards a patient. In fact, he'd gone out of his way to put Becca at her ease on Saturday. It had been a surprise at the time, and Alison had found herself thinking about it more than once over the weekend. After reading all those articles in the magazines, she'd expected Jack to be full of his own importance, but he wasn't like that at all.

It was exactly the same when it came to his son, too. It was obvious how much he cared about little Freddie, and that wasn't what she had expected either. So which was the real Jack Tremayne? The handsome playboy surgeon who devoted his free time to partying, or the dedicated doctor and father?

She wished she knew, because it might help her decide how she felt about him. If she could slip Jack into one category or the other, it would make her life so much simpler.

Nick decided to walk down to the harbour after he finished surgery. It had been a busy morning and they'd been hard pushed to keep on top of all the work. It was a good job that Adam Donnelly had decided to take a permanent position with the practice, he thought, otherwise they would never have coped now that Marco had left. Although he was glad that Lucy didn't intend to rush back to full-time work, they definitely missed her.

He walked along Harbour Road until he came to the lifeboat station and stopped. It was a cold, crisp day, the sun sparkling off the water. Shading his eyes, he peered out to sea, feeling the ache of loneliness nagging at him harder than ever that day. He missed Annabel, and still felt guilty about the way she had died. He should have paid more attention to what had been happening at home, instead of focusing all his energy on his job. If he'd done that then maybe his children would want to spend more time with him now, too, and he wouldn't feel so alone.

He was glad that he had made his peace with Lucy, but the situation between him and Jack was no better. He needed to find a way to get through to him, but after what had happened on Saturday he was even more wary of putting his foot in it. Maybe he and Jack were destined to remain at loggerheads. The thought was dispiriting.

'Penny for them?'

Nick swung round when he heard a familiar voice, summoning a smile when he saw Kate Althorp. He had missed Kate since she'd left the practice, missed their chats and missed seeing her around the place. However, he knew in his heart that it was better that she'd left. There was no chance of them ever being more than friends, and he didn't like to think that he was holding her back. He wanted Kate to be happy because she certainly deserved to be.

'Hello, Kate. How are you?'

'Fine, thanks. How about you?' She gave him a gentle smile. 'You looked deep in thought when I spotted you just now.'

'I was.' Nick sighed. 'I was thinking about Jack.'

Kate's pretty face clouded. 'Don't tell me that you two still haven't sorted out your differences.'

'I'm afraid not.'

'You need to make your peace with him, Nick. I know that you two have had problems in the past, but surely it's time you put all that behind you. Jack needs your help now more than ever.'

'He brought Freddie into the surgery on Saturday,' Nick said wistfully.

'To see you?' Kate said hopefully.

'No. The poor little mite had been running a temperature and was feeling very out of sorts. Jack brought him in to be checked over. He had no idea I'd be there. In fact, I got the distinct impression that he wished one of the others had been on duty.'

'But at least he asked you to see Freddie,' Kate pointed out. 'That has to be a step in the right direction.'

'Maybe.'

Kate laid her hand on his arm. 'I hate to see you tearing yourself apart like this, Nick. It isn't right.'

'It isn't what I want, believe me.' He put his hand over Kate's. 'I want to be friends with my children, not feel that I'm their worst enemy.'

'Then do something about it!' Kate removed her hand and stepped back. 'All right, so it won't be easy, and it won't happen overnight either, but if it's what you really want then you will find a way, Nick. Right, that's the end of my peptalk. I'd better get on and do my shopping.'

She gave him a quick smile, then headed along the road. Nick watched until she disappeared from view, then turned and stared out to sea. Could he and Jack resolve their differences? He wanted to believe they could, but he couldn't do it on his own—Jack would have to meet him halfway. And he wasn't sure if his son was willing to make the effort.

CHAPTER FIVE

'Right, Becca, I want to check how those cuts I stitched on Saturday are doing. If you can swing your feet over the side of the bed so that you're facing me...that's great.'

Jack smiled at the teenager as he pulled up a chair. It was Monday afternoon and he had just finished a ward round. Alex had been called away to see a patient and Jack had been left in charge of the team. He had deliberately omitted Becca from the round because he understood how traumatic she would find it to have so many people gathered around her. Now he grinned conspiratorially at her.

'The rest of the guys wanted to meet you, but I decided to keep you to myself for a while longer. Is that OK?'

'Yes.' The girl gave him a wobbly smile. 'I was dreading having everyone staring at me.'

'No way is that going to happen, sweetheart,' Jack said firmly.

He leant forward and carefully examined her face, using a magnifying lens so that he could see the more severely injured areas better. The cut on her forehead was healing well, although it might not appear so to the untutored eye. However, Jack had spent the last five years of his life—two as a senior house officer, doing his basic surgical training, followed by three of the allotted six years needed to gain his certificate of completion of training—looking at injuries such as this, and it didn't faze him. The skin wasn't inflamed, there was no puckering, and no sign of necrosis in the surrounding tissue either. He was confident that it would leave only the smallest of scars in time, and told Becca that.

'Are you sure? You're not just saying that because it's what you think I want to hear?'

'It doesn't work like that, Becca. I shall always tell you the truth, so if I say there won't be much scarring, it's because I know that for a fact.'

'Oh. I see.' Becca gulped. 'What about the rest of the cuts? Will they leave a lot of scars?'

'They're healing well. This one here on the edge of your jaw might leave a bit more of a scar, but even that shouldn't be too bad.' Jack smiled at her. 'It takes time for the scar tissue to settle down and fade, but I'm confident that your face will look fine eventually. And any areas you aren't happy with can be covered up with make-up—you'll be shown how to do that after your treatment has finished.'

'What about the big cut on my left cheek? Is it going to need a skin graft?'

'Yes, it is.' Jack sat back in the chair, knowing that he needed to explain exactly what would happen without frightening her. 'Do you know what happens when skin is grafted?'

'Not really.' Becca pulled a face. 'I've never thought about it.'

'Of course you haven't. Nobody does until they need to have one done,' Jack assured her. 'Basically, there are two types of graft—split thickness and full thickness. I will need to use a full-thickness graft on your cheek because the match will be better, and that's very important.'

'You said you would take the skin from behind my ear,' Becca reminded him, and he laughed.

'Go to the top of the class for remembering that! Most people don't remember a word they're told after an accident, and no wonder either.'

He carried on when Becca laughed, pleased to see that she was looking a little more relaxed. It would be an ordeal for anyone to have to face this type of surgery and it must be doubly difficult for a teenage girl.

'I shall remove a small section of skin from behind your ear, slightly larger than the area it needs to cover to allow for shrinkage. I'll have to put a couple of stitches into the site from where I take the graft, but it will heal pretty quickly and shouldn't cause any problems. Once I have the graft, I will fit it precisely over the area on your cheek and make sure it's securely attached. You'll need to wear a pressure bandage on it for a while afterwards to keep it flat, but that's basically it.'

'And will everyone be able to tell that it's a graft? I mean, will it look different to the rest of my face?'

'There's bound to be some scarring,' Jack explained gently. 'But the results are usually excellent. In a year or so, you will hardly notice it at all.'

'A year!' Becca sounded stricken. 'It will take that long to heal?'

'It could do.' Jack leant forward and looked her straight in the eyes. 'I know it's going to be hard, sweetheart, but I promise you that you will hardly notice any difference in time.'

'But I'll still look like a freak when I start university this October,' she wailed.

Jack tried to console her, but nothing he said calmed her down. In the end, he wrote her up for a mild sedative and went to have a word with her parents who had arrived back from holiday that morning. They too were distraught when he explained the situation to them, and that made him feel worse. He wished with all his heart that there was something more he could do, but he couldn't perform miracles. All he had was his skill as a surgeon, and in some cases it simply wasn't enough.

A cloud of gloom seemed to hang over him for the rest of the day. He checked on Becca before he left, but she was very subdued and barely responded when he spoke to her. He drove back to Penhally Bay and collected Freddie from the nursery, and it seemed fitting that his son was in an equally downbeat mood.

He took Freddie home and made his tea, then phoned Lucy for a chat, but he could tell that he'd caught her at a bad moment so he didn't stay on the phone very long. Freddie was playing with some of his toys, but he turned away when Jack knelt down beside him. He sighed. It seemed that he was persona non grata wherever he went today.

He was heading to the kitchen to make himself a cup of coffee in the hope it would chase away the blues when the doorbell rang, so he veered off to answer it and was surprised when he found Alison standing outside. She had Sam with her and she looked unusually serious.

'I'm sorry to disturb you but I've just discovered that Sam has nits.'

'Nits?' Jack repeated blankly.

'Yes. One of the other mums told me that she'd found some in her little girl's hair when I collected Sam from the nursery at lunchtime, so I made a point of checking.' She grimaced. 'Apparently, he and Freddie were playing together this morning so I thought I'd better warn you. Once one child gets them, they spread like wildfire.'

'Oh, I see. Well, thanks for telling me.'

'That's all right.' She turned to leave, but all of a sudden Jack knew that he couldn't bear to spend the evening with only his thoughts for company.

'What do you recommend to get rid of them?' he said hurriedly. He shrugged when she glanced back. 'I'm not very clued up on head lice, so is it best to buy something from the chemist? Malathion is used in most of the patented lotions, I believe'

'It is, although I'm not too keen on using such strong chemicals. Whenever I've come across a case at work, I've always recommended conditioner.'

'Hair conditioner, you mean?' Jack's brows drew together. 'Does that really work?'

'Oh, yes. If you apply a thick layer of conditioner to Freddie's hair after you wash it then you can comb any lice or nits out with a fine-toothed comb.'

'That sounds a better option than dousing his head in chemicals. Thanks for the tip. As you've probably guessed, this is all very new to me,' he added wryly.

Alison raised her eyebrows. 'I'll bet it is. Checking your son's hair for nits isn't how you would usually spend your evenings.'

'What do you mean?' Jack asked, somewhat puzzled by the comment.

'Nothing. Forget I said anything.'

She turned to leave again, but he had no intention of letting her go without an explanation. He opened the door wider and stepped back.

'I can't forget it now that you've said it, can I? Why don't you come in and tell me over a cup of coffee exactly how I should be spending my evenings. I was just about to put the kettle on when you rang the bell,' he added when she hesitated.

'I really can't see the point,' she began, but Jack was having none of it. If she had something to say then he wanted to hear it. For some reason he didn't understand, he didn't want her getting the wrong idea about him.

'Then do it as a favour. I was sitting here feeling very sorry for myself when you rang the bell, and I could do with cheering up.'

'Has something happened with Freddie?' she asked anxiously as she stepped into the hall.

'Yes and no.' He shrugged, wondering how to explain that he was feeling rejected because his son hadn't wanted to play with him.

'Hmm, that sounds ambiguous enough to be intriguing,' Alison said lightly. She unzipped Sam's coat, then ushered him into the sitting room. 'Go and play with Freddie while Jack and I make some coffee, darling. I'll be in the kitchen if you need me.'

Jack headed to the kitchen and filled the kettle as the two boys settled down to play with some building blocks. Alison followed him in, grimacing as she took stock of the tired units and chipped worktops.

'I thought my kitchen was bad, but this is a mess. It looks as though it could do with a complete make-over.'

'Tell me about it.' Jack scooped coffee into the cafetière. 'The whole place needs refurbishing. It's having the time to get it sorted out that's the biggest problem.'

'Are you going to do it? I thought you'd only rented the cottage?'

'Yes and no.' He grinned at her. 'That's becoming my favourite answer, isn't it? Sorry. I don't mean to be so vague. It's just that everything about my life seems to be up in the air at the moment. It's hard to give you a definite answer.'

'It can't have been easy for you, uprooting your life and moving down here,' she said, sitting down. 'I mean, you've left your home and all your friends—no wonder it feels as though your life is in turmoil when you've had to make so many changes.'

'It's not that, exactly.'

He sat down opposite her, feeling his heart give the strangest little flutter when she looked at him with her hazel eyes full of sympathy. Few people had felt the need to sympathise with him. He wouldn't have thanked them if they had. He prided himself on the fact that he could take care of himself and didn't need anyone to prop him up, yet it was different when he was with Alison; he felt differently around her.

He chased away that thought and smiled at her, falling back on the charm that had got him through so many tricky situations in the past. 'I enjoyed living in London, and I doubt I'd have moved away if it hadn't been for Freddie. But as for missing my friends—well, that really isn't a major factor.'

'Are you sure? After all, you led a very hectic social life when you lived in the capital. It's understandable if you feel bored and restless now that you've moved out here.'

'Ah! Obviously you read all the rubbish that was written about me a few years ago,' Jack said ruefully. He held out his hands, palms up. 'What can I say? I had a great time and I enjoyed all the parties, et cetera, but it was only ever one small part of my life. I grew out of that whole scene some time ago, and I don't miss it either.'

'No?'

'No,' he said firmly when he realised that she didn't believe him. 'There's only so much partying a person can do before it becomes boring. You see the same old faces wherever you go, have the same pointless conversations. It might appear like a fabulous way to live to anyone watching but it's not really like that, believe me.'

'Then why did you do it if you didn't enjoy it?'

'Oh, I enjoyed it well enough in the beginning,' he admitted. 'Going to all those exciting new places and meeting people you've only ever seen on television or at the cinema gives you a tremendous buzz at first. Most people find themselves swept away by the glamour of it all.'

'As you were?'

'Yes.' He sighed. 'I went a bit mad when I first moved to London—fell in with a crowd whose main aim in life was to enjoy themselves. If I hadn't had my work then heaven knows what would have happened. It's what stopped me going off the rails. Especially after I met India.'

'That's when most of the articles appeared,' Alison said softly. She blushed when he looked at her in surprise. 'I used to buy a lot of the gossip magazines, and you and India featured prominently in them.'

'You don't strike me as the sort of person who reads stuff like that,' Jack said, getting up to pour the coffee. He took the mugs back to the table then fetched the milk and sat down again.

'Normally I wouldn't read them, but I was going through a difficult time. They seemed to fill a gap in my life, if that doesn't sound too silly.'

'Of course it doesn't sound silly!' He put his hand over hers and gently squeezed it, felt his breath catch in the most alarming fashion, and hastily released her. 'If they helped, great. Don't feel guilty about it.'

He picked up his mug and took a sip of the scalding-hot brew. He wasn't going to ask her why her life had been particularly difficult at that point, not if he hoped to keep a grip on his wayward emotions. He was already stressed because of what had happened with Becca and Freddie, and he didn't think he could cope with anything else—like getting upset on Alison's behalf.

'I don't.'

She lifted the mug to her lips and blew on the coffee to cool it, and Jack felt his insides bunch themselves into knots as he watched her lips purse. From what he could tell, she wasn't wearing a scrap of lipstick, but she didn't need it to enhance the pouty fullness of her mouth.

Tingles suddenly started to shoot through his body, flashes of electricity that charged every cell, and he buried his face in the steaming mug. He had slept with a number of women in his time, kissed a hell of a lot more and flirted with probably triple that number, but at no time could he recall feeling as keyed-up as he felt right now. The sight of Alison's lush bare mouth was playing havoc with his senses, stirring them into a bubbling cauldron of desire. He wanted to lean across the table and kiss her, run the tip of his tongue over those soft, delicious lips and taste them, then gently— ever so gently—nibble the lower one. And that was just for starters!

Jack shot to his feet, mumbling something about checking on the boys because it was the first excuse his overloaded brain dredged up. He almost ran out of the kitchen, praying that Alison didn't suspect what was going on. He couldn't imagine that she would, not when he was having such difficulty accepting the concept.

He leant against the wall and groaned. This *couldn't* be happening. He couldn't be having lustful thoughts about a woman he barely knew, a woman, to boot, who apparently believed he was some kind of…of dissolute *playboy*. It was mad, senseless, stupid, ridiculous and every other adjective in between. It simply couldn't happen. He wouldn't allow it to!

He took a deep breath and turned to go back into the kitchen, then felt the floor ripple beneath his feet when he caught sight of Alison. She was drinking her coffee, and all the feelings he'd experienced before seemed to multiply tenfold as he watched her. He couldn't drag his eyes away from her mouth as it neared the cup—a small purse of her lips, a tiny puff of cool air, followed by a tentative sip. It was like poetry in motion and he would have been happy to recite the verse for the rest of his life—purse, puff, sip.

Jack quickly closed his eyes. He had no idea what was going on but he had enough to contend with: a child who was so traumatised he wouldn't speak; problems with his father; a demanding job. He didn't need or *want* to add anything else to the equation. He had to stop watching Alison and lusting after her, and get a grip!

Alison put down the cup and looked around the kitchen. It really was a mess, she decided, and if she'd had to live here she would have had to do something about it.

Her gaze skimmed over the cabinets, which had been painted in a particularly vile shade of green, and she shuddered. No wonder Jack was finding it hard to settle into his new life when he had to live in a place like this. Compared to what he had left behind in London—all that glitz and glamour—it must be a shock. Maybe he claimed that he was over the party scene, but she couldn't believe he didn't miss all the rest.

It made her wonder how long he would stay in Penhally Bay. She couldn't see him spending the rest of his life in this quiet little backwater—it was simply a stopgap. At the moment he needed his family's help to look after Freddie, but once he got used to being a father he would move on, probably return to London and jump right back into the social scene.

It was what Sam's father, Gareth, had done. He had been brought up in London and had missed city life when he had moved to Cornwall to work. Although Alison had realised when she'd met him that he'd found country living boring, she'd hoped he would adapt in time. When she'd discovered she was pregnant, she'd thought it would help Gareth to put down roots, but it hadn't worked out that way.

After Sam had been born the situation had grown worse. Gareth hadn't coped with either the responsibility of being a father or the restrictions of having a new baby to look after. He had left her for another woman when Sam had been six months old and returned to his former life in the city. She'd had no contact with him since. It was upsetting to compare Jack with Gareth and realise they had so much in common.

'More coffee?'

Jack came back into the kitchen and she started nervously. She shook her head, hoping he couldn't tell how unsettled she felt. It shouldn't make a scrap of difference whether Jack stayed in Cornwall or left, but it did.

'Sure?' He picked up the cafetière and held it, poised, over her cup.

'No, this is fine. Thank you,' she added belatedly.

Jack topped up his mug and sat down, stretching his long legs under the table and accidentally kicking her foot. 'Sorry,' he murmured as he lifted the cup to his mouth.

'It's OK,' Alison replied, tucking her feet safely out of the way.

She picked up her own mug, feeling very ill at ease all of a sudden. It had been some time since she'd thought about her ex-husband, and it was worrying to wonder why she had thought about him now. She'd steered clear of relationships since the divorce. It hadn't been difficult when she'd been so busy looking after Sam and earning enough money to keep them, but there'd been a couple of occasions when she'd been asked out on a date. Each time she had refused.

Although she hadn't ruled out the idea of meeting someone else, she was wary of making another mistake. If she ever got involved again with a man, she would need a cast-iron guarantee that he wasn't going to let her down. And a man like Jack Tremayne definitely didn't come with a warranty. Any woman who got involved with him wouldn't know what to expect—in or out of bed.

The thought made her blush and she rushed into speech. 'How are the boys—?'

'The boys are fine—'

They both spoke at once and both stopped. Jack grinned at her. 'Ladies first.'

'I was just going to ask if Sam and Freddie were all right.'

'They're fine. They're playing some sort of complicated game involving lots of cars and building blocks.' Jack put his mug on the table and sighed. 'At least Freddie seems to enjoy playing with Sam. He completely blanked me when I offered to play with him earlier. He didn't want anything to do with me, in fact.'

'He's probably still feeling very unsettled,' Alison said quietly, thinking that the son took after his father in that respect. It was obvious how unsettled Jack was feeling, and the thought simply compounded all her fears about the dangers of getting involved with him.

'That's what I keep telling myself.' Jack gave her a quick smile, then changed the subject. 'So what would you do with this place if you lived here?'

'It would depend how long I was planning on staying,' Alison said cautiously. 'It isn't worth spending a huge amount of money if it's only a temporary arrangement, is it?'

'Bearing in mind how hard it is to find somewhere to live around here, I can't see myself moving in the foreseeable future.'

'No?' She shrugged, clamping down on the bubble of happiness that had popped up inside her because Jack wasn't planning on leaving.

'No. The whole point of coming back here was so that

Freddie would have his family around him. I'm certainly not thinking about uprooting him again for a very long time.'

'In that case, I suppose it depends what you're allowed to do. The cottage is a holiday let, isn't it? There must be restrictions on what tenants can do to the property.'

'It was a holiday let, but it's been taken off the market now.' Jack shrugged. 'It's owned by a subsidiary company of Whitethorn Holidays.'

'India's family business?' Alison exclaimed.

'It was. Now it all belongs to Freddie.'

'You mean that Freddie inherited the company after India died?'

'Yep. The whole kit and caboodle.' Jack waved a hand around the kitchen. 'Including this place. India was an only child, and she left everything in trust to Freddie. He'll come into his inheritance when he's twenty-five, although there's money set aside for his use before then—for school fees, university, that kind of thing.'

'I had no idea,' Alison admitted.

'That's because I don't want people making a song and dance about it.' Jack's expression was sombre. 'I want Freddie to grow up like any normal kid and not be burdened by the fact that he's so wealthy. I firmly believe it was that which led to India going off the rails, and there is no way that I'm going to let the same thing happen to Freddie.'

Alison nodded. 'I agree. I know that everyone thinks it must be great to be really, really rich, but it must be a huge liability at times.'

'I'm sure it is. Don't get me wrong—money is important and I'm not decrying the fact. You need enough to live comfortably, but after that...' He shrugged. 'It can cause an awful lot of problems, from what I've seen. That's why I don't intend to touch any of Freddie's money. I earn enough to keep us and that's it.'

Alison admired the stance he'd taken and said so. 'Not many people would feel that way, Jack.'

'Maybe not, but it's how I feel. My only concession is this cottage. We needed a place to live, so I decided to rent it with a view to buying it in the future if it proves suitable for our needs.'

'Which is why you don't mind refurbishing the place?' she suggested, and he grinned at her.

'Got it one! So, come along, let's hear your ideas for turning this place into a proper home.'

The next hour flew past as Alison did exactly that. It was only when Sam came to find her because he was thirsty that she realised how late it was. She jumped to her feet, groaning as she glanced at her watch.

'I got so carried away that I didn't realise the time. You should have stopped me.'

'No way. I need someone to set me on the right track.' Jack stood up and smiled at her, a lazy, boyish smile that made her bones melt. 'I'm not really strong on the home-making scene, and it's good to be able to crib your ideas.'

Alison chuckled as she took Sam into the sitting room and put on his coat. 'I'm no expert when it comes to interior design, so don't go by me. I'm sure you can find someone better qualified to advise you.'

'You mean a *real* interior designer?' Jack said, making imaginary speech marks with his fingers. He shuddered. 'No, thanks. I don't want the place looking like something out of a trendy magazine. I want it to be proper home, a place where Freddie can play and not have to worry about making a mess.'

'Well, you should get that all right. There's a lot of mess when you have a three-year-old,' she said, looking pointedly at the sitting-room floor, which was littered with toys.

Jack laughed. 'I don't care so long as he's happy.' He

looked at his son and an expression of sadness crossed his face. 'That's all I want for him—to be happy.'

'And he will be, Jack,' Alison said quietly, moved by the sadness in his voice.

'Let's hope so.'

He didn't say anything else as he showed them out, but Alison knew that he was wondering if he would ever fulfil his wish to make his son's life better. She wished she could help him but there was very little she could do.

It would have been different if she and Jack had been seeing each other, she thought as she and Sam walked home, then inwardly recoiled. She could never get romantically involved with Jack. Apart from the fact that he wouldn't be interested in someone like her, she wouldn't risk her heart being broken a second time. She and Sam were better off on their own. And as for Jack—well, he would manage perfectly well without her help.

CHAPTER SIX

JACK had just dropped off to sleep when he heard the phone ringing. Rolling over, he grabbed hold of the receiver before the noise woke Freddie. 'Jack Tremayne.'

'Jack, it's Alex Ross. I'm sorry to wake you but we have a full-scale alert on so we're having to call in every available member of staff.'

'What's happened?' Jack demanded, dragging himself out from under the duvet.

'A light plane has crashed on Bodmin moor. The pilot declared an emergency and Air Traffic Control advised him to set down on the A30. Apparently the police were trying to clear the road when it happened.'

Jack's heart sank. 'Do I take it the plane hit a car?'

'A minibus bringing a group of sixth-formers back from a geography field trip.' Alex said. 'It was absolute carnage, from what I can gather. Incident Control has asked us to take the burns cases, which is why I need you in here, pronto.'

'I'll be there just as soon as I can.'

Jack hung up and leapt out of bed, wondering what he was going to do about Freddie. He could take him with him, but then what? He couldn't just dump the child in the hospital and go merrily about his business.

He dragged on a shirt and a sweater, finger-combed his hair, and headed for the stairs, still mulling over his options.

He could phone Lucy and ask her to have Freddie, but it was gone midnight and he hated to wake her up when she had the baby to look after. Alison was another possibility, but he was even warier about taking that option after what had happened that evening.

His brain made a lightning-fast detour to that moment when he had watched Alison drinking her coffee and he sucked in his breath. This is neither the time nor the place for that, Jack, my lad, he told himself sternly.

He reached the bottom of the stairs and paused as he stared at the phone sitting on the table beside the front door. If he wasn't prepared to ask either Lucy or Alison for help, then who could he phone?

He groaned softly. There was really only one other option—one he wouldn't have considered if he hadn't been desperate. Picking up the receiver, Jack punched in the number, steeling himself when he heard the person on the other end pick up.

'Dad, it's me—Jack. Look, I'm sorry to bother you at this time of the night but I need a favour.'

'Jack, good to see you.'

Jack grinned at his brother-in-law, Ben Carter. 'So you got roped in as well?'

'I was already here when it all kicked off so I stayed on to help.' Ben grimaced. 'It's a bad one. There's a lot of kids injured, as well as the people on the plane.'

'I thought we were only getting the burns injuries?' Jack said quietly, following Ben to the resuscitation room, where the very worst cases were being treated.

'So did I. However, it appears there was another major accident tonight outside Launceston, involving a coach and a lorry. Every A and E unit for miles around is chock-a-block. Incident Control decided that we would take the most seriously injured from the plane crash and the rest would be ferried round to anywhere that has room for them.'

'What a mess!' Jack exclaimed.

He followed Ben into Resus, feeling the adrenaline start pumping around his body at the scene that greeted him. Every available bed was being used and the place was buzzing. He swung round when he heard the high-pitched whine of a monitor going off.

'He's arrested,' somebody shouted, and Ben groaned.

'That's the pilot. It doesn't look good, I'm afraid.' He pointed over to where screens had been placed around one of the beds. 'Alex is over there. OK?'

'Fine.'

Jack made his way across the room and slipped behind the screens, smiling when Alex looked up. 'Looks like a fun time is being had by all.'

'You could say that,' she agreed dryly.

Jack's expression sobered as he looked down at the teenage boy who was lying on the bed. The left side of his face had been burned, although it was difficult to tell how badly damaged the skin was without a closer examination. However, it was obvious that there was severe burning to his upper left arm, and Jack knew without having to check that it would need a lot of work to sort it out. He glanced at Alex and raised his brows.

'Ryan Lovelace, aged eighteen, a passenger in the minibus,' she explained crisply, leaning over to adjust the drip attached to Ryan's uninjured arm. One of the major factors in burns cases was shock caused by the rapid loss of large quantities of fluid from the affected areas, so Jack appreciated why Alex was so keen to ensure that the boy's fluid levels were restored as quickly as possible.

'Apparently he got out of the minibus, but he went back to help some of the others, and that's how he got burned.'

'I see.' Jack smiled at the boy. 'That was a brave thing to do, Ryan.'

'Naw, anyone would have done the same,' Ryan said dismissively.

Jack doubted it, but he didn't argue with him—he was more concerned about the severity of his injuries. Bending down, he examined Ryan's face first. There was some blistering, but most of the dermis—the deeper layer of the skin—appeared to be unscathed. That was good news because it meant there should be less scarring once the area healed.

It was very different with the boy's upper arm, however. The burns to this area were third-degree burns. The full thickness of the skin had been destroyed and there was a section of muscle exposed. Although the worst damage was confined to a relatively small area, that didn't mean it wasn't a significant injury. Skin acted as a barrier to prevent airborne infection getting into the body, and once it was breached bacteria could rapidly infiltrate the tissues.

'I take it he's on broad-spec antibiotics?' he said, glancing at Alex.

'Yes. I got him started on them immediately.'

'Good.' Jack frowned. 'I'd like to get him to Theatre as soon as possible. What's the schedule like?'

'Chaotic,' Alex said. 'I'm waiting for a slot for one of the passengers in the plane—he's got third-degree burns to both hands. Ben has a girl who needs her leg amputated—she's being prepped at the moment, and he'll be going back to her as soon as he's finished with the pilot. Then there's another three who need glass removed from their faces. I'm not sure if they need theatre time as I haven't had a chance to assess them yet.'

'That's quite a queue, even without them,' Jack said wryly.

He arched a brow. 'What do you suggest we do—toss a coin to see who gets theatre space?'

'It might come to that,' Alex warned him, smiling. 'We're still waiting for another couple of casualties to arrive, too. The helicopter is bringing them in, and we won't really know what we're dealing with until it gets here.'

Jack shook his head. 'I thought it was bad in London, but it's no better here.'

'No. Sadly enough, accidents happen in even the quietest places—'

Alex broke off when one of the nurses came over to her. She turned to Jack. 'Theatre two is free, so that's me sorted. Are you happy to deal with this case on your own?'

'Yes, so long as you're happy to leave it to me,' Jack confirmed.

'Oh, I have no worries on that score. Right, I'll see you later. You know where I am if you need me.'

Jack returned his attention to his patient once Alex left. Pulling on some gloves, he carefully examined the boy's face. He liked to have an overall picture of the problems before he actually did anything. He checked Ryan's arm as well, and knew that his initial assessment had been correct: it would need reconstructive work to ensure the muscle wasn't adversely affected, and skin grafts to help it heal.

There was still no sign of a slot in Theatre becoming vacant after he had finished assessing Ryan's injuries so, rather than waste time, he took one of the teenagers who'd got glass in his face into the treatment room and sorted him out in there.

Using a high-powered magnifying glass, and working under local anaesthetic, he was able to remove the slivers of glass. A couple of tiny sutures, a light dressing and the boy was free to leave. Jack took him through to the waiting room and had a word with his parents, explaining that the stitches could be removed at their GP's surgery rather than at the hospital. He hadn't realised until the parents told him they were patients of his father that some of the school kids came from Penhally Bay. The accident would have a big impact on the town.

It was his turn for Theatre then, so Jack didn't have time to dwell on it. However, as he made his way to the changing room, he couldn't help wondering what Nick would think of his work when he saw the youngster.

He sighed. Alex was confident enough about his abilities to leave him to get on with the job, so his father's opinion shouldn't matter, but it would be good to have his approval for once. Still, at least Nick had agreed to look after Freddie for him, and that had to be a step in the right direction.

Maybe it was the fact that he was a father himself now, but Jack suddenly found himself hoping that he and Nick would be able to resolve their differences in time. All it needed was for Nick to meet him halfway and they could start being a proper family again—Dad, Lucy, Ben, Annabel, Ed, Freddie and him.

Just for a moment another name flashed into his head, but he blanked it out. Alison wasn't part of this equation and there was no point hoping that she ever would be.

Alison heard about the accident when she took Sam into nursery the following morning. Several of the mums were talking about it as it appeared there'd been a number of children from Penhally Bay involved.

By the time she arrived at the surgery, she knew that at least three of the injured teenagers were patients there. Sue, the receptionist, greeted her with a sigh when she walked in.

'I suppose you've heard the news?'

'About the crash? Yes, I have. From what I can gather, several of the kids are from here, too.'

'That's right.' Sue reeled off their names. 'Ryan Lovelace is the most badly injured. I met Mandy Lovelace on my way here—she's Ryan's aunt, you know—and she told me that he's got burns on his face and his arm. Apparently he got them dragging some of the other kids out of the bus.'

'Really? That was very brave of him!' Alison exclaimed.

'Wasn't it? It just goes to show there must be good in some branches of that family after all.'

Alison didn't say anything. Some members of the Lovelace family were patients at the surgery. Although it was widely known that they had their problems, she didn't feel happy about discussing them and diplomatically changed the subject. 'Are the children being treated at St Piran's?'

'Oh, yes. They took all the casualties there, so it must have been bedlam. Mandy told me that Jack operated on Ryan so he must have been called in.' Sue reached for the phone when it began to ring. 'I wonder what he did about his little boy?'

'I've no idea.'

Alison left Sue to deal with the call. Picking up the stack of notes that had been left in her tray, she made her way to the nurse's room, thinking about what Sue had told her. Had Jack asked Lucy to look after Freddie for him? She could only assume he must have done.

That was one of the drawbacks of him working at the hospital, of course. He would be on call any time the situation warranted it. It must make it very difficult for him to organise child care. Just for a moment she wondered if she should tell him that he could call on her if he was stuck, before she thought better of it. While she would be happy to help, she wouldn't want Jack to think there was an ulterior motive to her offer. He was so handsome and so charismatic that a lot of women must have pursued him over the years, and she would hate it if he thought that was what she was doing.

She frowned because that wasn't the only reason, of course. Normally she would have dismissed her qualms and made the offer anyway. However, she was too aware of the dangers of getting involved with him. She knew it would take very little for her to fall for Jack, and fall hard, too. And that was a risk she wasn't prepared to take.

It was lunchtime before Jack left the hospital. He had spent most of his time in Theatre, first of all sorting out Ryan's problems as much as he could, and then assisting Alex. Two of the passengers as well as the pilot from the plane had died, but the third man had survived. His hands had been badly burned, though, and Jack knew that, despite everything he and Alex had achieved, it was only the tip of a very big iceberg. It would need a lot more work to restore full use of the man's hands.

The injured teenagers had fared rather better. All except two had been discharged. Ryan would need skin grafts once Jack had a better idea what was going on in the underlying tissue, while Ben's patient—the girl who'd needed an amputation—would be kept in the orthopaedic ward. It could have been much worse, he decided as he got into his car to drive back to Penhally Bay, but it would also have been much better if the crash had never happened.

He drove home and took a shower, then headed to the nursery to check on Freddie. His father had left a message with the theatre staff to say that he was taking Freddie to nursery as usual that day, but Jack wanted to make sure his son was all right. He parked across the road and got out of the car, stepping back as a motorcycle whizzed past with its horn blaring. It was his fault for not looking what he was doing and it gave him a shock. He was just catching his breath when Alison hurried over to him.

'Are you all right?'

'Just.' Jack grimaced. 'I'm a bit spaced out after pulling an all-nighter, but that's no excuse. It was a stupid thing to do.'

'You should be more careful,' she admonished, and he grinned.

'Yes, miss.'

Alison chuckled. 'Sorry. I seem to have my bossy hat on today.'

'Don't worry about it. I could do with someone bossing me around at the moment. I'm completely pooped.'

He unlocked the gate and held it open for her to precede him, feeling his muscles clench when she brushed against him as she passed through the narrow opening. Maybe he was tired, he thought ruefully, but certain bits of him were in fine fettle.

'Did Lucy have Freddie for you last night?'

Thankfully, Alison seemed oblivious to his response, so Jack pulled himself together. 'No. I didn't like to phone her, seeing as it was so late. I asked my dad if he'd babysit for me. He came over to mine and stayed the night, then brought Freddie into nursery this morning.'

'Oh, that was kind of him. Mind you, he probably enjoyed it. It gave him a chance to spend some time with his grandson.'

'I imagine so,' Jack said, feeling guilty about the fact that he hadn't made any effort to invite Nick round before. OK, so his father had met Freddie at the surgery, but that hadn't been a social call. Apart from that, his son had had no contact with his grandfather until last night, and it really wasn't good enough.

'Did I say something to upset you?' Alison said anxiously.

Jack shook his head. 'It wasn't you. I just realised how remiss I've been by not getting Dad and Freddie together.' He shrugged. 'It's no secret that we have a rather rocky relationship, but I should have made more of an effort.'

'You haven't had much free time since you came back,' she pointed out.

'That's no excuse. I should have sorted something out.'

She touched his arm briefly. 'You're not Superman, Jack. You can only be in one place at any one time. Anyway, I'm sure Nick understands how difficult it is to juggle work and everything else.'

'I hope so.'

Jack smiled, because he didn't want her to worry any more about his problems. He rang the bell and waited for a member of staff to admit them. Most of the children stayed all day at the nursery, so there were only a couple of other parents there. He and Alison signed in, then went to the room where the three-year-olds were playing. Trish Atkins, the nursery nurse in charge of the children, came hurrying over to him.

'I'm glad you're here, Dr Tremayne. Did you get my message?'

'What message?' Jack asked, his stomach sinking as he looked around the room. There was no sign of Freddie, and he felt panic well up inside him as he wondered what had happened to him.

'I left a message on your home phone,' Trish informed him. 'Freddie has been very upset this morning and I thought I should let you know.'

'Upset? About what?' Jack demanded.

'I've no idea because he won't tell me,' Trish explained, looking worried.

'Was he upset when my father brought him in?' Jack demanded. Waking up to find a virtual stranger in the house must have been scary for the child, and he should have thought about that, although he had no idea what he could have done about it in the circumstances.

'He seemed a little subdued, but he's usually very quiet so it wasn't unusual. He wasn't crying, though,' Trish added.

'Where is he now?' Jack said.

'One of the staff is sitting in the quiet room with him. We thought it was best if we kept him away from the others in case he upset them, too.'

Jack followed her through a door at the far end of the room, his heart aching when he saw his son curled up on a mat in the corner, sobbing his little heart out. He hurried across the room and scooped him into his arms. 'Hey, tiger, what's wrong?'

Freddie took a gulping breath as he wrapped his arms tightly around Jack's neck. Jack could feel him shuddering as he lifted him up. 'It's OK,' he crooned, kissing the top of his head. 'Daddy's here and he won't let anything hurt you.'

Freddie was inconsolable as he clung to him, and Jack was at a loss to know what to do. He desperately wanted to comfort him, but he didn't know where to start. His gaze went to Alison, who had followed him into the room, and his heart caught again when he saw the expression on her face. Alison understood how powerless he felt, and realising it seemed to unleash all his fears.

Up till now he had been putting on a brave face, but he needed help if he was to get through to Freddie. Although he did his best, he didn't have any experience of dealing with such a young child. He had been thrown in at the deep end when he had taken custody of Freddie. He hadn't had time to learn how to be a good father to him, but if he didn't get it right he would *never* build a proper relationship with his son. The thought scared him to death.

Jack took a deep breath as panic gripped him. He needed help and he needed it now. Although he could ask Lucy's advice, she was in much the same boat as him. She was a new parent, too, and she was just learning what having a child was all about. His father was the next best option but, bearing in mind their already strained relationship, Jack didn't want to go down that route. That left him with just one other choice—one he wasn't sure if he should consider.

His gaze rested on Alison as he felt a sudden tightening in his chest. Could he ask Alison for help? *Should* he ask her when he was experiencing all these strange ideas about her? He would hate to think that he might solve one problem only to find himself with an even bigger one on his hands.

CHAPTER SEVEN

ALISON could have wept when she saw the anguish on Jack's face as he cradled Freddie in his arms. Hurrying forward, she put her hand on his arm. 'Let's take him home. He's far too upset to stay here for the rest of the day.'

'You're right.'

Jack tried to smile, but she could tell the effort it cost him and her heart went out to him. She squeezed his arm, wanting him to know that she understood how he felt. 'I'll just fetch Sam and then we'll leave.'

She went back to the playroom and found Sam. He skipped along beside her as they left the nursery, and his joyful attitude was such a contrast to Freddie's obvious unhappiness that it made her see something had to be done. When they reached the road she turned to Jack.

'Would you like to come home with us? It might help to take Freddie's mind off whatever is bothering him if he plays with Sam for a while.'

'Are you sure you don't mind?' Jack said hesitantly. 'It seems like such an imposition…'

'Rubbish! Of course it isn't an imposition. In fact, I insist you come back and have some lunch. It's my half-day off because I'm working on Saturday morning, so I don't need to go back to the surgery, if that's what you're worried about. To be frank, you're in no fit state to cope on your own.'

'It's that obvious?' Jack gave her the ghost of his usual multi-megawatt smile. 'I don't think I could punch my way out of a paper bag at this precise moment, to be honest.'

'No wonder, after the night you've had,' she said sympathetically.

Jack sighed as they crossed the road. 'If it was just tiredness, I could cope. It's seeing Freddie like this which is so hard to deal with. I don't know what to do for the best to help him.'

'I understand how difficult it is, Jack, but you have to hang in there.' She glanced at the little boy and lowered her voice. 'Freddie needs you. That's obvious from the way he's clinging to you.'

'It is, isn't it?' Jack said wonderingly. He turned to her and she saw tears welling in his eyes. 'It's the first time he's ever shown any sign of affection towards me.'

'Then it's a real breakthrough. Just hold onto that thought.'

She waited while Jack unlocked his car. Fortunately, there was a built-in child seat in the rear armrest so there was no question of Sam not being safely strapped in. Jack got Freddie settled, then slid into the driving seat. He started the engine, then glanced in the rear-view mirror.

'Freddie seems a bit calmer now, doesn't he?'

'He does. He just needs time to get over whatever it was that upset him and he'll be fine.'

'I just wish I knew what started it all off,' Jack said flatly. 'I feel as though I'm stumbling about in the dark all the time because he won't talk to me.'

'He will eventually,' she said encouragingly. 'He just needs time and a lot of love.'

Jack didn't say anything, but she could tell he wasn't convinced the solution was so simple. Maybe it wasn't that simple, but she was sure that what Freddie needed most of all was love, and Jack seemed to have an abundance of that when it came to his son. Whether he had enough love to spare for a woman as well was another matter. From what she had gleaned from all those press reports, he seemed to be commitment-phobic. He fell in love, and fell out of it again even faster.

She sighed. Jack's love life had nothing to do with her. Although she was happy to help him with Freddie, she wasn't going to make the mistake of getting involved with him on a personal level.

By the time they arrived at Alison's house Freddie seemed much calmer. Jack carried him inside and took off his coat. He frowned as he watched his son run over and kneel down beside Sam. 'He looks much happier now, doesn't he?'

'Yes, he does. And he'll look even better after he's had something to eat. You, too,' she added, heading for the kitchen.

'Are you sure you don't mind feeding us?' Jack followed her, but the kitchen was only big enough to accommodate one person comfortably so he propped himself against the door rather than crowd her.

'Of course I don't mind!' She opened a cupboard and took out a couple of tins. 'Beans on toast all right?'

'Lovely,' he said fervently, then grinned when she looked at him in surprise. 'I've had nothing to eat since last night, so beans on toast sounds like manna from heaven to my poor empty stomach.'

'First time I've heard them described as that,' she said lightly.

Jack watched as she found a pan to heat the beans, then cut some bread for the toast. He had never mastered the art of cooking, and he admired the way she seemed so at home in the kitchen. 'I never seem to get the timing right.

Either the toast is cold by the time the beans are ready or vice versa.'

'It's just practice.' She buttered the toast and piled the beans on top, then handed him two of the plates. 'These are for the boys, if you could take them through.'

'Right you are.'

Jack took the plates in and put them on the table, then went back for the cutlery. Alison handed him the knives and forks, then picked up the other two plates.

'I'll bring these in.'

Jack laid the table, then called the boys over. Sam immediately climbed onto a chair, but Freddie didn't look too sure about the arrangements. Pulling out a chair, Jack bent down so that he was at eye level with him.

'You can sit on this chair or on my knee, Freddie. It's up to you.'

The little boy glanced at Sam, then scrambled onto the chair. Jack smiled at him as he pushed him closer to the table. 'Good boy.'

Jack sat down and tucked into his own meal, wolfing down the food as though his life depended on it. He was so hungry that he couldn't remember a meal ever tasting so good, and said so.

Alison laughed. 'What about all those wonderful meals you had in London?'

'Vastly overrated. Forget the champagne and caviar. I prefer good old baked beans on toast any day of the week!'

'If you expect me to believe that, you must think I'm really gullible.' She started to gather up the plates, but Jack took them from her.

'I'll do that. You cooked, so it's only fair that I do the washing-up.'

'There's no need,' she protested, following him to the kitchen.

'Of course there is.' He put the plates in the sink and turned on the taps. 'Where do you keep the washing-up liquid?'

'In here.'

She reached around him to open the cupboard door at the same moment as Jack turned. His body brushed up hard against hers and every cell suddenly went on the alert. He could feel the softness of her breasts pressing against the wall of his chest and froze.

'Sorry.'

There was a breathy quality to her voice that sent the blood rushing to his head and he bit back a moan. Another second of this torture and he wouldn't be held responsible for his actions!

'Here you are.'

Alison shoved a bottle of detergent into his hands and hastily retreated. Jack's head cleared as though by magic. He added a squirt of detergent to the water and plunged his hands in, yelping when he discovered how hot it was.

'Have you scalded yourself? Let me see.'

Suddenly Alison was behind him, her breasts nudging his shoulderblade as she tried to peer around him, and Jack gulped in air like a drowning man. There was only so much temptation a man could stand and he was well past his limit.

'I'm fine,' he said gruffly.

'Are you sure?' She leant forward, unconsciously piling on the agony as her breasts flattened themselves against his back.

'Quite sure,' he said, hoping she couldn't hear the panic in his voice. 'Would you mind checking on Freddie for me? I don't want him thinking he's been abandoned again.'

'Oh, yes, of course.'

She hurried from the kitchen and Jack was left on his own. Picking up a plate, he sluiced it in the hot water, wishing he could wash away the feelings that were rioting around inside him. He couldn't recall feeling so aroused before in his life, and couldn't understand why he felt this way. Was it the fact that he hadn't had sex for months that was causing the problem? he wondered suddenly.

Since Freddie had appeared on the scene he hadn't had time to think about his sex life. It hadn't been a priority before that either, because he'd been devoting every waking minute to his career. In fact, thinking back, it must be over six months since he'd been out with a woman, and closer to a year since he'd slept with anyone.

It was a shock to realise that, although it did help to explain why he was so responsive when he was around Alison. Jack breathed a sigh of relief as he finished washing the dishes. It had been scary to think there was something special about Alison when the answer was actually so mundane.

He dried his hands and went back to the sitting room. Alison was kneeling on the floor, playing with the boys. She laughed when Sam crashed his toy car into a tower of plastic blocks and sent them skittering across the floor, but Jack didn't join in. The blood was pounding inside his head again, and pounding through other parts of his body as well. Maybe the lack of sex was a contributing factor, but it was hard to believe it was the only reason he felt this way. What if it *was* Alison who was making him feel like this? What if he was falling in love with her?

A couple of months ago Jack would have scoffed at the idea of him falling in love, but he would have scoffed at the idea of him being a father, too. As he had discovered to his cost, life didn't follow a plan—it kept throwing up obstacles, and the trick was not to trip over them. He had avoided love in the past, but who said he could continue doing so?

The only guaranteed way he could avoid falling in love with Alison was to move away, and he couldn't do that because of Freddie. Freddie needed stability in his life; he needed people around him whom he could learn to trust. Jack couldn't uproot the child again. He had to stay here, and if that meant dealing with his feelings, that was what he would do. Freddie's needs would always come first.

'That's cheating!'

Alison grabbed hold of Sam and tickled him until he squealed with laughter. Glancing up, she felt her heart lurch when she saw Jack watching them. She had no idea what he was thinking at that moment, but he looked desperately unhappy. She gave Sam a final hug and stood up.

'How about you and Freddie doing some drawing for a change? If you clear away the cars, I'll find you some paper.' She headed to the door, nodding her thanks when Jack moved out of her way. 'I'll just get them settled down and then put some coffee on.'

'That would be great. Thanks.'

He gave her a quick smile, but she could see how strained he looked and it worried her. Jack was one of the most confident people she'd ever met, so why did he appear so ill at ease all of a sudden?

Alison mulled it over as she went into the kitchen for some paper and the felt-tipped pens. She had no idea why Jack was so on edge. She certainly couldn't think of anything she'd done to make him feel that way. In the end she decided that she was imagining things, so she got the boys settled and went to make the coffee.

Jack was slumped on the sofa when she got back. He

looked so worn out that her heart ached for him. He glanced round when he heard her come into the room and smiled.

'I was just about to nod off,' he explained, sitting up. He moved the coffee-table closer to the sofa, then took the tray from her.

'Power naps are the latest craze, I believe,' Alison told him lightly, kneeling down on the rug so she could pour the coffee.

'Power naps, eh? I must remember that if I'm caught on the hop in work,' he said, his blue eyes filling with laughter. 'It sounds much more professional than admitting that you're having forty winks!'

Alison chuckled. 'It certainly does. I believe all the City bankers are using the phrase to explain why they're asleep at their desks.'

'I don't blame them. If I had to spend my days poring over a lot of dusty old figures, I'd probably be taking power naps, too.'

The muscles in his arm flexed as he reached for the sugar, and she felt her heart bounce up and down a couple of times. She hurriedly stood up, refusing to allow herself too much leeway where Jack was concerned. Picking up her cup, she took it over to the chair and sat down, kicking off her shoes and tucking her feet beneath her. Jack murmured contentedly as he sipped some of his coffee, then leant back against the cushions.

'I think I'm just about coming back down to earth. It was a really busy night.'

'I believe Ryan Lovelace was one of the kids who were injured?' Alison said, cradling her cup in her hands.

'That's right. Apparently he went back into the bus to help his friends and that's how he got burned.'

'How bad is he?'

'The burn to his face should heal without leaving much

of a scar, but his left arm is a different story. There's some damage to the muscle as well as to the skin and the subcutaneous tissue. Muscle damage is extremely difficult to repair and it's going to take time to sort it all out.'

'What a shame! And after he was so brave, too.'

'I know. It doesn't seem fair, does it?' he said. 'Anyway, I've done some of the preliminary work, so that's a start, and I'm hoping to get another shot at it later this week. I need to see how much more tissue needs excising first. I've removed any that was obviously burned but there could be deterioration in the coming days and I might need to remove some more.'

'Will he regain full use of his arm?' Alison asked worriedly.

'If I don't need to remove too much more of the muscle. He'll need good physio, though, plus a lot of determination.'

'There's no problem on the physiotherapy score,' she assured him. 'Lauren Nightingale will soon get him sorted out.'

'Lauren's still here? Great! She's the best person I know when it comes to motivating a patient.'

Alison felt a little stab of jealousy assail her when she heard the warmth in his voice. She took a sip of her coffee, not wanting Jack to suspect that she harboured such feelings. Lauren was a first-rate physiotherapist, and the fact that she just happened to be extremely beautiful was of no consequence. She had no right to censor the people whom Jack liked.

The thought was so ridiculous that she gasped, and some of her coffee shot down the wrong way.

Jack looked at her in concern when she coughed. 'Are you all right?'

'Some coffee went down the wrong way,' she spluttered, trying to catch her breath.

Jack stood up and came over to her. 'I'll pat you on the back. It might help.'

Before Alison could protest, he started patting her back, and the rest of the air suddenly whooshed from her lungs. The feel of his strong hand between her shoulderblades was doing horrendous things to her, making her feel both hot and dizzy, and she choked.

'You really *are* in a bad way.'

There was real concern on Jack's face now as he bent over her. This close she could see the laughter lines fanning from the corners of his eyes, smell the clean scent of his skin and taste the coffee-scented warmth of his breath on her lips. It felt as though she was being immersed in sensations and she shuddered deeply.

'Here—let's give it another go.'

He started rubbing her back then, his strong hand caressing the length of her spine in a way that made Alison want to purr with pleasure, if only she'd had enough breath to spare. She could feel the heat of his palm seeping into her flesh, and for the first time in ages she felt desire rise up inside her. She stared up at him without saying a word and saw the exact moment when concern changed to something else, something hotter and wilder that couldn't be contained any longer.

When his head dipped, she closed her eyes, anticipating the moment when his mouth would claim hers. She could feel the feather-light brush of his lips as they hovered over hers and her heart overflowed with need. She wanted this kiss so much, needed it more than she had needed anything in such a long time…

He drew back abruptly, and her eyes flew open as she

stared at him in confusion. He gave her a tight little smile as he straightened up.

'That seems to have done the trick. Now I think it's time we left. Thank you for everything you've done today, Alison. I really appreciate it.'

'It was my pleasure,' she said stiffly, standing up.

She went over to the boys and quietly explained that it was time for Freddie to go home, and all the time she was doing so her heart was racing. Jack had been going to kiss her. She had no idea why he had changed his mind, but she knew it was what he had been going to do.

That fact should have been shocking enough, but what made it worse was knowing that she wouldn't have stopped him. Panic gripped her. If Jack had kissed her then she would have kissed him back, and to hell with the consequences.

CHAPTER EIGHT

WHAT on earth was wrong with him? He'd not only embarrassed himself by making a pass at Alison, but he'd embarrassed her as well.

Jack could barely contain his chagrin as he helped Freddie into his coat. He fixed a smile to his mouth as he turned to Alison, desperate to salvage some shred of his dignity. 'Thanks again for everything.'

'You're welcome.'

She saw him to the door, her own smile fixed just as firmly into place, but Jack could tell that she was upset. Although he was terrified of making the situation worse, he knew that he had to say something. He certainly didn't want her to think that he might come on to her again at the slightest excuse.

'About what happened just now—well, I'm sorry.' He shrugged, doing his best to hide how mortified he felt. He had always prided himself on being in control of his actions, yet he had come within a hair's breadth of ruining everything. 'I don't know what came over me. Put it down to the long night I had—obviously I'm not thinking clearly.'

'Don't worry about it. I shan't.'

Her smile held fast but the chill in her eyes cut him to the quick. Bearing in mind the rather unflattering picture she had formed of him initially, she probably thought he was a serial philanderer now, someone who couldn't keep his hands off a woman if she came within a ten-mile radius of him.

The thought stung because it wasn't true. It wasn't the fact that Alison was a woman that had affected him… Well, not *only* that, he amended truthfully. It was Alison herself, the person she was, that had made him want to kiss her.

It was impossible to explain that to her without digging himself an even deeper hole. Jack took the line of least resistance and beat a hasty retreat.

He took Freddie home and spent the rest of the day worrying about what he'd done. Whichever way he looked at it, it hadn't been a wise move at the moment. In a year or so's time it might have been a different story, of course. Once Freddie was more settled, and his own life had taken on some kind of proper structure, maybe he would have time for a spot of romance.

He frowned, because the thought of a little light romance didn't appeal to him. It might have been enough for him in the past, but it wasn't enough for him now. Not with Alison. He wanted to do more than just sleep with her. He wanted to sleep with her *and* wake up with her lying beside him in the morning. He wanted to know that he could do the same thing the next day and the day after that, too. In fact, there was a word for what he wanted, one he had steadfastly avoided:commitment.

Jack groaned as he got up and switched on the stereo, hoping the music would drown out any more dangerous ideas. He couldn't afford to waver at this point. He had to concentrate on Freddie and how he was going to help him. No matter how he felt about Alison, his son was his number-one concern.

Alison found it difficult to sleep that night. Every time she closed her eyes, she kept having flashbacks to the moment when Jack had been on the verge of kissing her. Consequently, she felt completely drained when she got up the next day, and it was an effort to get herself and Sam ready.

She dropped Sam off at the nursery earlier than usual so she wouldn't run into Jack, and went into work. Dragan Lovak, one of the doctors in the practice, was in the office when she arrived and he greeted her with a smile. Dragan had moved to England as a teenager to escape the war in Croatia. Alison had always found him to be very sympathetic towards his patients, and suspected that his past experiences had given him an insight into other people's suffering.

'Ah, Alison, just the person I wanted to see. I have a patient who has been diagnosed with diabetes. At the moment she's very unsure about giving herself daily injections of insulin and I feel that she needs some reassurance if she is going to be able to cope. I was wondering if you could teach her the best way to administer the injections.'

'Of course. Who is it?'

'Sophie Banks.' Dragan handed her the patient's file. 'She's just fifteen and it's a lot for her to deal with. I know it's short notice, but could you see her today? The sooner she accepts what has to be done, the better.'

'Let me check my list.' Alison brought up her list of appointments on the computer. 'I could squeeze her in at four o'clock, after the antenatal clinic finishes. Shall I get Sue to set up an appointment for her?'

'That would be wonderful. Thank you.'

Alison went through to Reception and had a word with Sue, who promised to phone Sophie's mother and make the arrangements. 'Are you going on Maggie's hen night?' Sue asked after she'd logged the appointment into the computer.

'I'm not sure.' Alison frowned. 'When is it?'

'Two weeks on Friday. Maggie says there is no way that she's having a hen party the night before her wedding, so she's booked it early.'

'I don't blame her!' Alison agreed with a laugh.

There'd been a lot of excitement when Adam Donnelly and Maggie Pascoe had announced that they were getting married at the end of the month. All the surgery staff had been invited to the wedding, as well as Maggie's friends and colleagues from St Piran Hospital. Would Jack be going? Alison wondered, then quickly erased the thought. She wasn't going to spend the whole day thinking about Jack!

'I'll have to wait and see if I can get a babysitter,' she explained, then glanced round when Gemma Johnson, the young nurse who had recently joined the practice, came in. 'How about you, Gemma? Are you going to Maggie's hen night?'

'I most certainly am! In fact, I have something special planned to make the night go with a bit of a buzz,' the irrepressible Gemma confessed.

Alison groaned. 'I don't think I want to hear this. I'll wait until the night and worry about it then!'

She left Gemma and Sue discussing the arrangements and went upstairs. The morning flew past with the usual mix of people who needed to be seen. She was just about to put on her coat to fetch Sam from the nursery when she heard a commotion downstairs and hurried down to see what had happened.

Hazel was sitting on the floor outside the office, looking very shaken, and there was blood pouring from a cut on her right thigh. Alison was about to kneel down beside her when Nick arrived. He took one look at Hazel and turned to Alison.

'Fetch some bandages. We need to stop this bleeding.'

Alison flew into the supply room and grabbed a handful

of bandages out of a box. Ripping open one of the packets, she ran back and handed it to Nick, who was trying to stem the bleeding.

'Thanks. Let's lie her down first, and then I want you to continue applying pressure to the wound.'

They helped Hazel lie down on the floor, then Alison grasped her thigh, pressing firmly either side of the wound. Direct pressure flattened the blood vessels and slowed the rate of bleeding so that clots could form. However, continuous pressure needed to be maintained for up to fifteen minutes for it to be effective.

She also raised Hazel's leg and supported it on her knees, knowing it would help to control the flow of blood if she raised the limb above heart level, but the wound continued bleeding heavily. Nick shook his head as he wound a second bandage over the first one and bound it in place.

'It's going to need stitching and we can't do it here. It's far too deep.' He raised his voice and shouted to Sue. 'Can you phone for an ambulance, please? Hazel needs to go to St Piran.'

It took just ten minutes for the ambulance to arrive, and in the meantime they had to add another couple of bandages as the original ones became soaked through with blood. They also put a drip into Hazel's arm to compensate for the loss of fluid, because she was complaining of feeling cold and dizzy. However, Alison was relieved when the paramedics lifted her onto a stretcher. She turned to Nick as the crew wheeled Hazel to the door.

'I'd like to go with her, if it's OK with you. Gemma can cover the antenatal clinic this afternoon. She's sat in with me a couple of times so she knows what to do. It will be good practice for her.'

'Fine,' Nick agreed. 'I'd go myself but I have to stay here

in case anything else crops up. Take a taxi back when you've finished and charge it to the surgery.'

Alison hurriedly asked Sue to phone Carol, the child-minder, and ask her to collect Sam from nursery, then grabbed her coat. She climbed into the back of the ambu-lance and held Hazel's hand as they drove to the hospital.

'I feel such a fool,' Hazel said weakly. 'I was only open-ing a new carton of stationery and the knife slipped...' She gulped back a sob. 'Dr Tremayne must think I'm useless for causing such a fuss.'

'Don't be silly. It could have happened to anyone,' Alison assured her.

They drew up outside A and E and she followed as Hazel was wheeled through to the treatment area. Fortunately, she was deemed a priority case, so it didn't take very long before she was seen. It was the same registrar Alison had met when she'd accompanied Becca, and he grinned when he recognised her.

'Doing another good deed, I see.'

Alison laughed. 'Something like that.'

He let her stay while he examined Hazel. As Nick had said, the cut was deep, and Alison could tell the registrar wasn't happy with it. He got one of the nurses to clean it up, frowning when he took another look at it through a high-powered magnifying lens.

'The vein's been nicked—that's why there's so much blood. I'll have to get one of the surgical team down here because it's too fiddly for us to repair.'

Alison nodded, too busy trying to control the lump that was rapidly forming in her throat to reply. She had a horrible feeling that she knew who would respond to the call, and her heart sank as she considered how it might look. Would Jack think that she had offered to accompany Hazel so she could see him?

It was immaterial what he thought, of course. She couldn't abandon Hazel now. However, her heart started racing when she heard footsteps in the corridor. Was it anticipation or fear that made it pound so hard? she wondered. Or a bit of both? She wanted to see Jack again, and there was no point pretending otherwise, yet she knew that she was getting in way over her head. All she could hope was that her natural caution would stand her in good stead. But when the curtain swished back she knew that all the caution in the world wasn't going to protect her. Just seeing Jack again made all thoughts of being sensible fly right out of her head.

Jack was surprised when he saw Alison sitting beside the bed, but he was determined that he wasn't going to let her know how he felt. He smiled at her as he drew the curtain shut behind him.

'Been drumming up more business for us, have you?'

'It's all my fault,' Hazel said before Alison could reply. 'I'm really sorry, Jack. You have enough to do without me being so stupid.'

'There's nothing to apologise for, Hazel,' he said firmly. 'These things happen, so don't beat yourself up about it. Now, let's have a look and see what you've done.'

He took a fresh pair of gloves out of the box, nodding his thanks when Alison moved out of his way. Bending down, he carefully examined the wound on Hazel's thigh, determined to blot out everything else so he could focus on what needed to be done. He wasn't going to let the fact that he could smell the fresh apple scent of Alison's shampoo affect him. No, siree! Neither was he going to pay any heed to the fact that he could hear her breathing. And as for the fact that her face seemed to be dancing before his eyes, well, he would sort that out PDQ! He'd spent the night torturing himself for his sins and he deserved a reprieve.

Jack made himself breathe slowly, in and out, and gradually his concentration returned. On closer examination he could see that the iliac vein—the large vein in the leg which ran parallel to the femoral artery—had been nicked. It would need to be repaired by microsurgery or it would continue to bleed. Peeling off the gloves, he set about explaining it all to Hazel.

'I'm going to whiz you up to Theatre, Hazel. The vein's been nicked, and although it's not been completely severed it needs sewing up to stop it bleeding. I'll also need to put a few stitches in your leg—roughly ten should suffice, but don't hold me to that, will you?'

'Will I have to have an anaesthetic?' Hazel asked, obviously shocked by the thought of having an operation.

'Yes. You'll be given a general anaesthetic so you won't know what's going on.' He grinned at her. 'It also means you'll be spared the headache if I decide to sing.'

'Sing?' Hazel repeated blankly.

'Oh, yes. There's nothing like the acoustics in an operating theatre to bring out the performer in me.' Jack winked at her and she laughed.

'Get away with you! You always were a torment, even when you were a little boy.'

'Don't tell anyone or you'll ruin my image,' he implored her, hamming it up for all he was worth. It seemed his efforts to cheer her up had worked, however. She looked a lot more relaxed and that was what he'd been aiming for. He smiled at her again as he opened the curtain. 'I'll just go and check if there's a theatre free.'

He left the cubicle, feeling rather pleased with himself. Not only had he cheered up Hazel but he'd more or less managed to ignore Alison after that initial hiccup. If he could keep it up, he would soon be back on track.

A quick phone call soon elicited the information that

Theatre two would be available in approximately twenty minutes' time. Jack booked Hazel in, then went back and explained what was happening. Once he'd arranged for a porter to take her to be prepped, he was free until he was needed in Theatre.

He decided that he had time to grab a cup of coffee so long as he was quick about it. He headed for the coffee-shop in the foyer, because it was quicker than trailing all the way to the staff canteen, and bought himself a large cappuccino complete with chocolate sprinkles on the top and a biscotti on the side.

He had just sat down to drink it when he spotted Alison coming into the café and he groaned because it left him in rather a quandary. If he ignored her, it could send out the completely wrong signals. He didn't want there to be an atmosphere whenever they ran into each other, as they were bound to do. However, neither did he want her to think that he was coming onto her after yesterday. The question now was should he or shouldn't he invite her to sit with him?

Alison would never have gone into the coffee-shop if she'd had any idea that Jack would be there. When she spotted him sitting at a table in the corner her first instinct was to leave, only it appeared he had seen her. Her heart sank when she saw him beckon to her. She really didn't want to sit with him, but neither did she want him to know how much that near kiss had affected her.

In the end pride won. There was simply no way that she was going to let him think that she was bothered by what had happened. She bought herself a cup of coffee, then crossed the room. Jack greeted her with a smile as she approached his table, but she could see the wariness in his eyes and realised that he was as jumpy as she was. Why? Did he think that she was in hot pursuit of him, perhaps?

The thought set light to her temper. Pulling out a chair, she sat down. If Jack had got it into his head that she found him irresistible, then it was time she set him straight!

'I see you had the same idea as me.'

'Really?' Alison glowered at him. 'And what idea would that be?'

'Coffee, of course.' He frowned. 'Why? What did you think I meant?'

'Nothing.' Alison felt her face suffuse with heat and hurriedly picked up her cup.

'Why do I get the feeling that I'm missing something?' Jack said softly. He leant forward so that she was forced to look at him, and she felt her heart lurch when she saw how serious he looked. 'If there's something you want to say, Alison, then tell me. I hate it when there's an atmosphere brewing.'

'Of course there isn't an atmosphere. You're imagining things.'

Jack sighed. 'No, I'm not. I can tell that you're very uptight about something. If it's what happened yesterday, then I can only apologise again. I don't want us falling out over something so stupid as that.'

Alison bit her lip. She knew that she should deny it was that nearly-kiss that was bothering her, but she couldn't bring herself to lie to him. 'It's partly that. But it's mainly the fact that I don't want you thinking that I'm…well, *chasing* you.'

'Chasing me?' He looked at her in bewilderment. 'It never crossed my mind. Why on earth did you think it would?'

'Oh, I don't know. The fact that I accompanied Hazel here this morning…' She tailed off, wishing she hadn't said anything. It was obvious that Jack had never imagined she might be interested in him. Why should he have done when he clearly wasn't interested in her, as he'd been at pains to point out? What was it he'd said yesterday? That he'd been tired after the busy night he'd had and hadn't been thinking clearly? He couldn't have made his feelings any plainer than that.

Alison pushed back her chair. She couldn't bear to sit there a second longer and know what a fool she'd been. 'I have to go. I've just remembered there's an antenatal clinic this afternoon and I need to get back to the surgery.'

She knew she was gabbling, but it was preferable to admitting that she was disappointed because Jack hadn't really wanted her. She had just fulfilled a few basic criteria— young, female, available.

Pain lanced through her as she hurried to the door. She heard Jack call her name but she ignored him. She certainly wasn't going to let Jack know how devastated she felt because he would have responded the same way to any woman.

There was a taxi dropping off a fare so she asked the driver to take her back to the surgery. And all the way there she could feel the weight of her own stupidity pressing down on her. What made it doubly painful was that she'd made the same mistake once before, thought that she was someone worth loving, someone special.

Sam's father had shown her how wrong she'd been. He had found another woman to replace her and it would be exactly the same with Jack. He might enjoy the odd kiss, but he would soon grow tired of her, as Gareth had done.

A single tear trickled down her cheek and she wiped it away. There would be no tears and no wishing that things might have been different. She would accept that she'd made a mistake and put it behind her. Jack meant nothing to her. And she most definitely meant nothing to him.

CHAPTER NINE

Jack hurried to the door, but by the time he got there Alison was getting into a cab. He could only stand and watch as it drove away. He couldn't go after her when he was due in Theatre, and anyway what could he have said? That not even for a second had he imagined that she might be interested in him?

He made his way back inside, struggling to get to grips with the idea. She'd done nothing to make him think that she was attracted to him—apart from not pushing him away when he had almost kissed her, of course.

Jack stopped dead. Up till then he had blamed himself for what had happened, but was he solely at fault? Alison could have stopped him any time she'd wanted, but it had been he who had stopped, he who had realised the dangers of what they'd been doing. If he hadn't called a halt she would have let him kiss her and probably kissed him back.

The thought hit him with all the force of a bomb exploding. When his bleeper chirruped, he couldn't think what was happening at first. He hurriedly checked the display and discovered it was Theatre, calling to tell him they were ready for him. He headed for the lift, knowing that he didn't have time to think about the situation with Alison any more right then. But later, after he had finished work, he would need to decide what he was going to do.

* * *

The antenatal clinic was under way by the time Alison arrived back at the surgery. She popped her head round the door to let Nick know she was back and he quickly excused himself.

'How's Hazel?' he demanded, following her into the corridor.

'She needs surgery. Apparently the iliac vein had been nicked, and that's why we couldn't stop the bleeding. Jack said that he would keep her in overnight, but that she should be fine by the morning.'

'So Jack's doing the op, is he?' Nick asked.

'Yes.' Alison shrugged, desperately trying to keep a rein on her emotions. 'He responded to the call from A and E. I think Hazel was pleased he was going to do the op.'

'I'm sure she was. She's always had a soft spot for Jack. Like all the women around here,' Nick added wryly.

Alison couldn't think of anything to say. She knew it was true, and that was part of the trouble. Most women would be delighted to have Jack as their doctor, or as anything else for that matter. Fortunately, Nick didn't appear to expect a reply.

'I'd better get back. Gemma's coping extremely well, so we may as well let her carry on. You take a break now. You've earned it after all the rushing around you've done.'

'Thanks.'

Alison made her way to the staffroom and switched on the kettle. Normally she had her lunch at home, after collecting Sam from the nursery, and she didn't have anything with her to eat. She poked around in the cupboard and came up with half a packet of chocolate biscuits that had got shoved to the back. She had just made herself a cup of tea when Sue poked her head round the door.

'I'm sorry to disturb you, but Louise Appleton's in Reception. She's got Chloe with her and she wants to know if the poor little mite has chickenpox. Everyone's out on house calls except Nick, and I didn't know if I should disturb him.'

'I'll take a look at her,' Alison offered immediately.

She followed Sue back to the waiting room, smiling sympathetically when she saw Louise struggling to calm her fractious four-year-old daughter. 'Hello, Louise. I'm afraid all the doctors are out on calls at the moment, so shall I take a look at Chloe for you?'

'Please. I couldn't believe it when I saw the state of her. Her tummy is absolutely covered in spots!'

Louise looked harassed as she bounced the little girl on her knee. She was a single mother and had had Chloe while she had still been at school. Fortunately, once her parents had got over their shock, they had rallied round. With their support Louise had continued her studies after the baby had been born, and had earned herself a place at the local college where she'd studied floristry. Now she had her own shop on the outskirts of the town, and was doing extremely well, by all accounts.

Alison crouched down in front of them. 'Can I take a look at your tummy, Chloe? I promise I'll be quick.'

'No!' Chloe shrieked, pushing her hands away.

Louise apologised but Alison shook her head. 'Don't worry about it. She doesn't feel well, so it's understandable if she doesn't want people poking and prodding her. However, I think it might be better if we took her up to my room in case anyone comes in. I wouldn't like folk to think that we torture our patients in here!'

Louise laughed as she picked up her daughter and followed Alison up the stairs. It took a lot of cajoling, but in the end Chloe agreed to be examined. Alison nodded when she saw the small red spots that covered the child's torso.

'Yes, that's chickenpox. You'll probably find that the spots appear in crops—on her tummy, behind her ears, under her arms, maybe even in her mouth. They'll turn into blisters soon, and then dry up and form scabs.'

'What should I do about them?' Louise asked anxiously. 'I don't want her to be scarred, so is there anything I can use to help them heal?'

'The main thing is to stop Chloe scratching them. That's easier said than done because they can be very itchy. You need to cut her nails and keep dabbing the spots with calamine lotion—that usually helps. And do make sure that she doesn't pick at the scabs once they form. It can set off a secondary infection, and that's what causes the worst scarring.'

'Is there anything I can give her to make her more comfortable?'

'Just junior paracetamol if she's running a temperature,' Alison advised her. 'Most kids are a bit out of sorts for a couple of days, but they're not really ill. It's far worse for adults who get chickenpox, so I hope you've had it.'

'I'm not sure. My mum will know though. She kept a record of everything me and my sister Sarah had when we were children.' Louise grinned. 'I'm sure I'll never be that organised!'

'Me neither. Anyway, see how Chloe is tomorrow, and if you're at all worried about her, phone for an appointment.'

'I shall.' Louise stood up. 'How long will it take before it goes? I have to do the flowers for a couple of weddings next week, and it's going to make it difficult if Chloe can't go to the nursery.'

'It's roughly ten days before chickenpox runs its course, I'm afraid, and you'll have to keep her off school for at least that length of time.'

Louise grimaced. 'Oh, dear. Maybe my sister can look

after her if I'm stuck. Mum and Dad are going on a cruise at the weekend, and they won't be back until the middle of April.'

Alison frowned. 'Sarah's pregnant, isn't she?'

'Yes, she's just coming up to eight months. Why? Is that a problem?'

'It could be. Chickenpox can be quite dangerous to an unborn child if the mother is in the latter stages of pregnancy. Unless you're sure that Sarah has had it, I think you should keep Chloe away from her.'

'Oh, I will. What a good job you told me.' Louise picked up her daughter. 'Thanks, Alison. I really appreciate all the advice you've given me.'

'It's my pleasure.'

Alison saw them out, then went back to her tea, but it had gone cold by then. She emptied it down the drain and switched on the kettle again. Talking to Louise had given her a breathing space and helped her to get back on track after what had happened at the hospital. She felt a bit of a fool, in fact, for having run off like that, but there was no point dwelling on it. Anyway, she doubted if Jack cared one way or the other. He wasn't interested in her, and so long as she kept reminding herself of that fact, she wouldn't have a problem.

Jack went straight from Theatre to the afternoon ward round. Alex had made a start by the time he arrived, and she nodded when he explained where he'd been. They worked their way through the list until they came to Becca and Alex handed over to him.

Jack ran through the girl's case notes, so that everyone was up to speed, then knocked on the door of the side room and went in. He wasn't sure what kind of reception he would

receive. Becca had been very cool with him since he'd told
her how long it would take before her face healed, so it was
a nice surprise when she greeted him with a cheery smile.

'Hi, Dr Tremayne. How are you today?'

'Very well, thank you, Becca.' He waved a hand towards
the rest of the group. 'Is it OK if I bring the gang in to see
you?'

'Of course it is!'

She seemed in remarkably high spirits as he set about
examining her, and he found himself wondering what had
caused such a marked improvement in her mood. 'Everything
is looking great, Becca,' he told her after he'd finished.
'There's just your cheek to sort out, and I'm going to do
that tomorrow morning, exactly as we discussed.'

'Great. Will you be operating on me before Ryan?' She
grinned at him. 'I bet him that you'd do my op first and his
second, you see.'

'Did you, now?' Jack laughed as he realised what had
brought about the change in her attitude. There was nothing
better than a little attention from a member of the opposite
sex to cheer a person up. 'Well, I might have to think about
that.' He chuckled when she groaned. 'OK. You can tell
Ryan from me that you're first on my morning list.'

'Brilliant!' Becca whooped with delight and everyone
laughed. They all trooped out of the room but Jack hung
back.

'So what did you bet him? Something good, from the
sound of it.'

'Two tickets to a concert this summer. Whoever wins
gets to choose the show.' She beamed at him. 'That means
I'll get to choose it now.'

'I see.'

Jack sketched her a wave and left, thinking how simple

life was when you were that age. It was as you got older and took on more responsibilities that life became so complicated. That thought immediately reminded him of what had happened in the coffee-shop, and he sighed. The sensible side of him knew he should ignore it, but another side of him couldn't bear to let it go. If Alison was attracted to him then surely it was too good an opportunity to miss?

Saturday turned out to be a gloriously sunny day. Although Alison had been planning to catch up with some housework, the weather was far too nice to waste the day being stuck indoors. She decided to take Sam out for a picnic, so packed some lunch for them and set off in the car. It had been ages since she'd been to Rock, where she'd been born, and she headed in that direction.

The town was just coming back to life after the winter lull. There was quite a lot of traffic on the road, although it was nowhere near as busy as it would be once the season got under way. A lot of people had holiday homes in the town, and during July and August the place was packed. However, there were just enough people about that day to make it feel alive but not overly crowded.

Alison parked her car and headed for the harbour. Sam loved boats, and she knew he would enjoy watching the yachts. There was quite a stiff breeze blowing, and the tiny craft seemed to dance across the water, their brightly coloured sails bobbing about in the sunshine.

They sat down on the harbour wall while she unpacked a flask of coffee and a carton of squash for Sam. She helped him pierce a hole in the top of the carton with the plastic straw, then poured herself a cup of coffee, sighing in pleasure as she inhaled the fragrant aroma.

'That smells good. I don't suppose there's any to spare?'

Alison's head swivelled round and she gasped when she saw Jack standing behind her. 'What are you doing here?'

'Playing truant.' He grinned as he helped Freddie onto the wall. 'I'd made up my mind that I was going to decorate the house today. I had it all planned, too—I was going to start in the hall and work my way through all the rooms. But when I woke up and saw what a lovely day it was, I caved in. I'd *much* rather spend the day at the beach than up a ladder!'

'I know what you mean,' Alison conceded. 'I've got a stack of housework to do, but I couldn't bear to stay in when the sun was shining.'

'So you're skiving off, too? Great! It makes me feel a less guilty to know I'm not the only delinquent around here.'

He sat down beside her, his face breaking into a smile which immediately made her insides churn. He looked so handsome as he sat there with the sun bouncing sparks off his dark hair. He was dressed as casually as she was, in well-washed jeans and a navy-blue sweater over a pale blue shirt which brought out the sapphire colour of his eyes. A pair of disreputable trainers on his feet added to the picture of a man who was at ease with himself. Obviously Jack didn't feel that he had to dress up to impress. He didn't need expensive clothes to boost his ego either. He was comfortable in his own skin and it was something she admired about him.

Gareth had been very different. He'd spent a lot of time worrying about the impression he made, and the impression she made as well. He had been highly critical at times, so that she'd come to dread meeting his friends. He had continually compared her to the other women he'd met, and she had invariably come off worst, so it was little wonder her confidence had taken such a battering. However, she knew instinctively that Jack would never behave that way.

The thought was far too disturbing. Alison drove it from her mind as she reached for the flask. She topped up the cup and offered it to him.

'I'm afraid I haven't brought a spare cup with me.'

'Don't worry. I don't mind sharing.'

He lifted the cup to his mouth and her heart started to pound as she saw his lips touch the very same spot from where she had drunk a moment before. She turned away, busying herself with finding another carton of squash for Freddie. She'd made a fool of herself once before, and she didn't intend to repeat her mistakes again today.

'Here. It's your turn now.'

Jack handed her the cup and her heart started doing its yo-yo trick again. The thought of drinking from the cup after he'd used it made her feel very odd, but she could hardly refuse. She steeled herself as she raised it to her lips, wondering if it was the heat of the coffee that was making her mouth tingle this way. It was ridiculous to imagine that Jack's lips could have left an impression on the cup, although she couldn't remember experiencing such an odd sensation before.

By the time the coffee had been drunk, Alison was a bundle of nerves. Being with Jack was a strain, and there was no point pretending it wasn't. She was so aware of him that every cell in her body seemed to be humming with tension. When he stood up, she breathed a sigh of relief. He would probably thank her for the coffee and leave, no more keen to prolong this meeting than she was.

'Thanks for the coffee.'

'It was my pleasure,' she said politely, packing the flask into the picnic bag.

'Was it?' His voice was very deep all of a sudden, and her hands stilled. 'Was it really a pleasure, Alison, or are you just being polite?'

'Of course not!' She gave a tinkly little laugh that sounded false even to her ears, and Jack shook his head. Crouching down in front of her, he looked into her eyes.

'I made a complete hash of things the other day, didn't I? I upset you and, worse still, I made you feel uncomfortable around me. It was the last thing I intended to do, Alison, believe me.'

'It was my fault,' she said softly, glancing down.

'No, it wasn't.' He tipped up her chin so that she was forced to look at him. 'You told me the truth, and if anyone is at fault then it's me, not you. OK?'

She gave him a tentative smile. 'If you say so.'

'I do.' He straightened up. 'So, now that we've cleared up that misunderstanding, how about we spend the day together? It seems silly for us to go our separate ways when the boys are having such fun.'

Alison felt torn as she glanced at Sam and Freddie, who were happily playing with some of the pebbles that had been washed ashore. Although she was wary of agreeing to Jack's suggestion, she didn't want him to think that she was afraid to spend time with him. That would send out the completely wrong signals.

'Stop it.'

The quiet command made her jump, and she raised startled eyes to his face. 'What do you mean?'

'Stop worrying about what I might and might not think. I swear I don't believe that you've set your sights on me, Alison. Cross my heart and hope to die.' He grimaced. 'After all, I'm the one who made a pass at you. It's a wonder you didn't run for the hills as soon as I showed up today!'

Alison gave a small chuckle. 'There aren't that many hills around here,' she pointed out, her tongue firmly lodged in her cheek.

Jack rolled his eyes. 'I suppose I asked for that, but give a guy a break.' He held out his hands, palms up. 'Can I help it if I find you attractive?'

'Me?' She stared at him in astonishment. 'You find *me* attractive?'

'Of course.' He frowned. 'I'd have thought that was obvious from what happened.'

'But you said that you were tired and weren't thinking clearly…' She stopped, wondering if it had been wise to quote him.

Jack's expression darkened as he crouched down in front of her.

'And you took it to mean that it wasn't really you I was interested in,' he said silkily. 'That I'd have made a pass at any woman at that precise moment, in fact?'

She nodded mutely, afraid that anything she said would be too revealing. It had hurt to know that all she'd been to him was an available female body.

He sighed heavily. 'When I mess up, I do it big time, don't I?' He didn't give her time to answer before he carried on, and Alison's breath caught when she heard the emotion in his voice. 'Well, whatever impression I gave you the other day, Alison, it wasn't true. It was you I wanted to kiss. You and nobody else. Got it?' His voice dropped, sounding so husky and deep that she shivered. 'And it's you I want to kiss right now, too.'

He leant forward, and before she knew what was happening his mouth found hers. His lips were cool from the breeze and tasted faintly of salt. They were so delicious that she moaned a little with pleasure. Closing her eyes, she allowed herself to be swept away by the magic of the kiss. She could no longer hear the flapping of the sails, the clink of the yachts' rigging, the shouts of the people. All she could hear was her own heart beating as Jack plundered her mouth, but that was enough. For the first time in ages she felt wonderfully, gloriously alive. She wasn't a nobody any more, she was someone special—the woman Jack wanted to kiss!

CHAPTER TEN

JACK could feel his heart racing as he gulped in a tiny breath of air. It felt as though he'd just had an out-of-body experience, and he couldn't believe that a kiss could have had this effect on him. He had kissed a lot of women in his time, and enjoyed kissing them too, but kissing Alison had been a revelation. Quite frankly, that kiss had been better than full-blown sex!

He groaned as he went back for a second. He knew how dangerous it was to repeat the process, but he couldn't help himself. One kiss wasn't enough. He needed another, and knew he would need another after that. In fact, it would be easier if he started claiming these kisses in dozens. One dozen now, two dozen later, and so on and so forth. Even then he might never have his fill.

His lips closed over Alison's again and he sighed. Her lips were so soft and so smooth that it was sheer heaven to kiss her. She wasn't wearing any lipstick again that day, and he realised with a shiver of delight just how delicious the natural sweetness of a woman's mouth could be. His tongue flicked out as he tasted the delicate curve of her Cupid's bow, the fullness of her lower lip. When her mouth opened and gave him access to its inner sweetness, he groaned. Maybe he should start claiming these kisses in hundreds rather than mere dozens!

'Mummy, why are you kissing Jack?'

The shrill little voice burst the bubble of euphoria that had enclosed him. Jack drew back abruptly, his face flooding with heat when he found both Sam and Freddie watching them with undisguised interest. He had no idea how long the children had been standing there, but it was too long in his view. They were far too young to witness something like this.

'I…um…Jack and I are friends, darling. And sometimes friends like to kiss each other.'

Alison sounded breathless, but Jack didn't dare look at her to check. He needed to be sure that he had his emotions firmly under control before he took such a risk.

'Oh.' Sam looked at Freddie, then suddenly looped his arm around the other child's neck and planted a noisy kiss on his cheek. 'Freddie and I are friends, so that means I can kiss him, too, doesn't it?'

'I…er…well, yes, I suppose it does,' Alison said weakly.

Jack couldn't stop himself chuckling as the two boys happily went back to their game. 'Life is all black and white at their age, isn't it? There's no grey bits.'

'No.' She turned to him, her pretty face awash with colour. 'I think I've just made the situation even more confusing for them, though. Sorry. I didn't mean to mislead Freddie that way.'

'There's nothing to apologise for.' He took her hand and raised it to his lips, feeling her shudder in response as he pressed his mouth to the centre of her palm. It was an effort to stop there and not let his lips trail up the length of her arm. 'It was a great explanation. I certainly couldn't have come up with anything as good if I'd been put on the spot like that.'

'It wasn't true, though, was it?' she said, and he could tell that she felt guilty about misleading the children.

'It wasn't a lie either,' he said firmly, squeezing her hand. 'We are friends, aren't we, Alison?'

'Yes, of course we are.'

She gave him a tight smile as she freed her hand, and Jack could have kicked himself. He'd made it sound as though being her friend was all he was interested in, and it wasn't true. He wanted to be more than just a friend to her, a lot more. A *whole* lot more.

The strength of his feelings stunned him. He knew that he shouldn't be contemplating starting a relationship at the moment. Helping Freddie recover from the trauma he'd suffered was a full-time job, and he didn't have the time right now to spare for anyone else. It wouldn't be fair to expect Alison to hang around until he was able to devote some time to her, although there was no point pretending that he would find it easy to let her go either. In the short time that he'd known her she had come to mean a lot to him, and the thought of not being able to be with her was something he didn't want to contemplate.

He sighed. It might turn out that it would have to be friendship or nothing, and he knew what he would choose if it came down to it. But how would Alison feel about such an arrangement after those kisses they'd shared? Would she be happy to be his friend now that he had overstepped the boundaries of friendship? The thought that he might lose her because of his own stupidity was very hard to bear.

Alison picked up the empty squash cartons and sandwich wrappings and took them over to the bin. Jack and Freddie had shared their picnic, and now Jack was helping the boys to build a fort. At least it had helped to take the edge off the tension, although she still hadn't fully regained her composure.

She sighed as she stared across the harbour. She should

never have let Jack kiss her. All it had done had been to confuse the issue even more. There was no point pretending that she hadn't enjoyed the experience, though, when it had been a revelation to her.

She'd had little experience when she'd married Gareth, and she had blamed herself when their sexlife had turned out to be less than satisfactory. It had never occurred to her that it might have been her ex-husband's fault, but after what had happened just now she might have to reconsider. She had felt more during those few minutes while Jack had been kissing her than she'd felt the entire time she'd been married, and the thought shocked her. Surely she couldn't be falling in love with Jack?

The idea filled her with panic as she made her way back. She knew that she needed to get away from Jack and stay away from him, too. It was the only way that she would put an end to all these stupid ideas she kept having.

Jack glanced up when he heard her footsteps, and her heart sank when she saw the wariness in his eyes. Was he having second thoughts, too, wondering how he could ease himself out of a situation that wasn't to his liking? Maybe he had enjoyed kissing her, but the last thing Jack wanted was commitment. The thought spurred her on.

'I'm afraid I'm going to have to break up the party.' She smiled at the boys, avoiding looking in Jack's direction in case she weakened. She knew what she had to do and she mustn't allow herself to be sidetracked. Anyway, if Jack wanted a proper relationship with a woman, he would chose someone glamorous like Freddie's mother, not a dull little country mouse like her.

'It's time we went home, so say goodbye to Freddie, Sam. There's a good boy.'

Sam reluctantly obeyed, dragging his heels as he made his way over to her. It was obvious that he didn't want the day to end so soon, and she couldn't help feeling guilty about spoiling his fun. Just because she had problems keeping control of her emotions, it shouldn't mean that her son had to suffer.

'It's time we were going as well.' Jack stood up and rubbed his hands down his jeans to wipe away the sand. 'If I don't make a start on that decorating it will never get done. Come along, tiger, I'll give you a piggy-back.'

He lifted Freddie onto the wall, then bent down so the little boy could scramble onto his back. Once Freddie was safely settled, he turned to Alison. 'It's been really great today. Thanks for sharing your lunch with us. Next time I'll bring the picnic. OK?'

It was on the tip of her tongue to tell him there wouldn't be a next time, but she managed to hold back. Jack was only being polite; he wasn't seriously planning they should meet up again. If the truth be told, he was probably as keen as she was to avoid any complications.

They left the harbour and walked back through the town together. Jack stopped when they reached her car, his eyes very blue as he stared down at her. 'I enjoyed today, Alison. I hope you did too, and that what happened hasn't upset you.'

She gave a little shrug, and his jaw tightened. 'If I've made you feel at all uncomfortable, I can only apologise. Again!'

'You haven't...well, not really,' she amended honestly. She took a quick breath, then rushed on before her courage deserted her. 'I think it might be best if we steered clear of one another, though, don't you, Jack? Neither of us is in the market for a relationship, and I don't do affairs. I don't think I'm genetically programmed for them,' she added, to lighten the mood.

'I understand, and I think you're right, too. At the moment

I need to concentrate on Freddie. I simply don't have the time to spare for anything else.' He bent and kissed her softly on the cheek. 'I suggest we stick to being friends, if that's all right with you.'

'That's fine,' she said quickly, very much afraid that she was going to cry.

She unlocked her car and helped Sam climb into his seat. Jack gave her a crooked grin as he opened the driver's door for her to get in.

'Drive carefully. There's quite a bit of traffic on the road today, and a lot of these drivers aren't used to our narrow country lanes.'

'I'll take my time going back,' she assured him, starting the engine.

He slammed the door, then waved her out of the parking space after he'd checked for any oncoming traffic. Alison glanced in the rear-view mirror as she drove away and felt a lump come to her throat when she saw him walk over to his car. Even though he had Freddie with him, he looked so alone that it touched her heart.

In any other circumstance, she would have gone back and told him that she'd changed her mind about them avoiding each other. Jack needed all the help he could get, and she would have been more than happy to try and lighten his load. However, it was too risky to involve herself in his affairs. If she allowed Jack to become a part of her life, she would find it impossible to let him go. She couldn't bear to think that at some point her heart might get broken again.

The next week passed in a trice. Jack was so busy both in and out of work that he never seemed to have a minute to himself. He didn't complain, though, because it meant he had less time to brood about what had gone on between him and Alison.

Although he respected the decision she'd made, he couldn't pretend that he didn't miss her, especially when he dropped Freddie off at nursery each morning and she wasn't there. She'd obviously changed her routine to avoid bumping into him, and he missed their brief exchanges more than he would have believed. Several times he thought about phoning her to check that she was all right, but each time he stopped himself. As she had explained, she didn't do affairs, and he wasn't in a position to offer her anything else. It was easier for both of them if they kept their distance.

Thankfully, his working life was turning out to be a lot less stressful. Hazel had been sent home the day after her accident, but only after she had promised to rest her leg. Becca's skin graft had taken beautifully, and Jack was more than satisfied with the results. So long as there were no hitches, she would be discharged at the end of the week.

Ryan Lovelace's arm had been far more complicated, however. The muscle damage had been more extensive than Jack had hoped. Extra tissue had needed to be removed, and that had made the reconstruction process even more difficult. Ryan had been quite stoical when Jack had explained that he might never regain full movement in his arm. The boy had also accepted without a murmur that he would need intensive physiotherapy for some time to come.

Jack was so impressed by his attitude that he was more determined than ever to do everything he could for him. He contacted a former colleague in London who had a particular interest in that type of injury and arranged for Ryan to see him the following week. If there was someone better versed in this area he was willing to admit it, if it meant the boy had the best chance possible of making a good recovery. And if he worked hard, and learned all he could, one day other surgeons would refer patients to *him*.

He went into work on Friday morning and made straight

for the staffroom. Freddie had had a particularly bad night and it had taken ages to settle him down. Jack felt decidedly jaded, and a shot of coffee would be a welcome pick-me-up. He filled a mug, shuddering as the caffeine hit his system. Lilian, their SHO, happened to be passing, and she grinned when she heard him groan.

'It sounds as though you needed that!'

'I did. In fact, I could do with it served intravenously—it would hit the spot even quicker that way,' Jack replied, gulping down a second mouthful.

'Heavy night, was it?' Parkash said with a wink as he reached for the pot.

'Yes, but not in the way you imagine.' Jack leant against the edge of the table so he would be on hand to top up his cup. 'It wasn't wine, women and song that kept me up into the wee small hours, but one very unhappy little boy. Freddie had a really bad night and kept waking up all the time.'

Lilian grimaced. 'I don't know how people cope when they have kids. This job is stressful enough without having to factor in a family and all the problems that entails. I certainly couldn't do it.'

Jack shrugged. 'I felt much the same way. Kids definitely weren't on my agenda, so it was a bit of a shock when I found out I was a dad.'

'It must have been awful for you,' Lilian sympathised. 'Didn't you ever think of refusing to take on the responsibility for Freddie?'

'No way. The poor kid had been through enough without having his father abandon him as well. I couldn't have lived with myself if I'd done that,' Jack said truthfully.

'Then you must be a better person than me,' Lilian said wryly.

She let the subject drop, but the conversation stayed with Jack throughout the morning. It had never occurred to him not to take charge of Freddie. From the moment he had learned that he had a son, he'd known that he'd wanted to do everything possible to protect him.

Had Nick felt that way when he'd become a dad? he wondered suddenly. And was that why he had always seemed so demanding?

It was the first time that Jack had considered the idea, yet it seemed to fit. Nick wanted the best for his children and that was why he had been so hard on him, Lucy and Ed while they'd been growing up. It had been less a desire to rule their lives, as Jack had assumed, than a deep-seated desire to protect them from harm.

It was a revelation to see the situation through Nick's eyes. He could understand now why Nick had hounded him about his lifestyle when he'd moved to London. His father must have thought that he had been going completely off the rails when he'd read all that stuff in the press, and he, being stubborn, had done nothing to correct that impression.

He realised that he needed to speak to his father and resolve some of the issues that had sprung up over the years. It was Annabel's christening on Sunday, and that would be the perfect opportunity. It was time he made his peace with his father so they could both move on.

The decision seemed to lift his mood. Jack whizzed through the rest of the morning. He stopped for lunch, then did a stint in Theatre. It was quite a complicated case to repair damage caused when a skin cancer had been removed from an elderly woman's face. Effectively, it involved him giving the woman a face lift to avoid her face looking asymmetrical. When he had explained it to her, she'd been delighted at the thought of ending up looking several years younger.

As he worked away, Jack found himself smiling at the thought that something good had come out of a potential tragedy. It filled him with a renewed hope that he could do the same for Freddie—turn his son's life around and make him happy. If he could do that, he would feel that he had achieved something truly worthwhile.

His heart gave a sudden flip, because after that he could think about himself and what he needed. Maybe, just maybe, he wouldn't have to stay away from Alison for very long.

CHAPTER ELEVEN

ALISON studied herself in the mirror. It was Sunday morning, the day of Annabel's christening. She had got Sam ready first and left him watching a DVD, with strict instructions not to get himself dirty. Although she didn't usually spend a lot of time on her appearance, she'd wanted to make a special effort that day because Jack would be there.

She sighed. She knew how foolish it was to want to impress him. Leaving aside the fact that she'd decided to keep her distance from him, she had little hope of competing with the women he had known in the past. They certainly wouldn't have been wearing a dress that had been bought three years ago in a sale, neither would they have washed and dried their own hair. They probably had minions whose only purpose in life was to help them dazzle everyone when they went out!

She swung round, impatient with herself for behaving in such a ridiculous fashion. She was a grown woman and she should be past the age where she felt the need to impress people. As long as she looked presentable, that was the main thing.

She collected Sam and set off on foot for the church, because her car was at the garage, being serviced. Lucy had told her the christening would be held after the morning service finished, and she had timed her arrival to coincide with that. There were a lot of people milling about when she got there, so she led Sam to a quiet spot to wait for the rest of the party. Lucy and Ben arrived first with baby Annabel. They had Ben's cousin with them as she was one of the godmothers. Alison admired Annabel's christening robe, a gorgeous confection of cotton lawn and hand-made lace which, Lucy explained, had been handed down through the family.

Nick arrived next with Kate Althorp, the other godmother, hard on his heels. Kate had her son Jeremiah with her, and he immediately came over to play with Sam. There was no sign of Jack, and Alison felt her tension rising as she waited for him to appear. He was Annabel's godfather, and she couldn't imagine that he wouldn't show up. However, as the minutes ticked past, she could feel herself growing increasingly anxious. What if something had happened to him or Freddie?

The churchwarden had just asked everyone to move inside the church when he arrived. He looked grim as he hurried up the path with Freddie in his arms.

'Sorry I'm late,' he apologised, kissing Lucy on the cheek. 'We had a minor crisis and that held me up.'

'You got here and that's the main thing,' Lucy said cheerfully. She went to kiss Freddie, but the little boy immediately started screaming and she backed away.

'Sorry.' Jack apologised, his face looking very strained as he tried to quieten his son. 'He's really out of sorts today. Heaven knows what he'll be like when we go into the church. He'll probably scream the place down.'

Alison could hear the worry in his voice and knew that she had to do something to help. Leading Sam forward, she smiled at Freddie.

'Hi, Freddie. Would you like to play with Sam while your daddy helps Auntie Lucy?' She opened her bag and took out a couple of Sam's toy cars. 'You and Sam can play races with these cars if you want to.'

Freddie immediately stopped crying. The idea obviously met with his approval because he started struggling to be put down. Jack smiled at her as he placed him on his feet, and she felt something warm rush through her when she saw the gratitude in his eyes.

'Thank you so much. I've been tearing my hair out, imagining what was going to happen during the service. Are you sure you don't mind, though? It doesn't seem fair that you should be stuck outside.'

'Of course I don't mind.' She returned his smile, hoping he couldn't tell how glad she was to see him. Although it had been only a week since she'd seen him, she had missed him terribly. 'You go and do your bit. Freddie will be quite safe with me.'

'I know he will.'

Stepping forward, he dropped a kiss on her cheek, then hurried after Lucy. Alison took a deep breath when she felt ripples of heat start to spread throughout her body. It was just a token kiss stemming from gratitude, she told herself sternly. It certainly wasn't anything to get excited about.

Fortunately Sam demanded her attention at that point. He was thrilled to bits when he discovered that he wouldn't have to sit quietly in a pew. He and Freddie knelt down on the path and began a noisy game of chase with the toy cars. Alison smiled as she watched them. Although Freddie never said anything, he and Sam seemed able to communicate perfectly well.

An hour later everyone began to troop back out of the church. Ben and Lucy were having a christening party at their house, and most of the guests headed off in that direction. The church was almost empty when Jack came rushing outside, full of apologies.

'Sorry, sorry! Lucy wanted us to have our photos taken while we were all together.'

'It's fine, don't worry,' Alison assured him. 'Freddie's been fine. He hasn't cried once, in fact.'

'It must be your magic touch.' Jack sounded weary as he looked at his son. 'I've no idea what upset him today. I was upstairs getting ready when I heard him screaming, and he was inconsolable by the time I got to him. I honestly thought I'd have to phone Lucy and tell her I couldn't make it.'

'I wonder what upset him,' Alison said, frowning. 'What was he doing at the time?'

'Watching a film on the DVD player.' He shrugged. 'It was just a cartoon I bought on my way home from work on Friday. I can't see it was that which upset him.'

'Unless he'd seen it before and associated it with his mother,' she suggested, and Jack frowned.

'I never thought about that, although I know there were a stack of DVDs in the house when India died.' When he saw her surprise he elaborated. 'Her solicitor gave me an inventory of India's belongings after her house was cleared, and I remember noticing there were hundreds of DVDs on it. Everything was left to Freddie, so I had most of it put into storage. I didn't see the point of keeping things like DVDs, though, so I told the solicitor to give them to charity. Maybe I should have gone through them first.'

'You can't cover everything, Jack. Things are bound to crop up that remind Freddie of the past. You can't blame yourself because you don't know about them.'

'I suppose not.'

'There's no suppose about it. You're doing a wonderful job under very difficult circumstances and you have to remember that.'

'Yes, miss,' he replied with a grin.

Alison grimaced. 'Sorry. I didn't mean to sound so bossy.'

'Oh, I don't mind. I'm just glad that you've come up with such a sensible explanation for what happened. It stops me wondering what I've done wrong.'

'You've done nothing wrong. You're doing everything you can for Freddie.'

'Thank you.' Reaching out, he squeezed her hand. 'I really appreciate you saying that.'

'It's no more than the truth.'

Alison moved away when she felt a shimmer of heat ripple through her again. She couldn't believe how sensitive she was around him. Every time Jack touched her she reacted, and it was unsettling to know the effect he had on her. She gathered up the toy cars, then shooed the boys towards the lych gate. Jack paused under the thatched roof that covered the gateway.

'Do you need a lift to Lucy's? I can't see your car anywhere about.'

'It's at the garage, being serviced,' she admitted reluctantly, because she wasn't sure if it would be wise to accept his offer.

'I know we agreed to keep our distance, Alison, but it's only a lift,' he pointed out.

'I know,' she said quietly.

'But?'

'But one thing can lead to another if we're not careful.'

'Then we shall be extremely careful. Cross my heart and hope to die,' he added, making a cross over his heart.

She chuckled. 'That's going a bit far, don't you think?'

'Not if it puts your mind at rest.' He smiled at her. 'I've missed you this past week. Dropping Freddie off at nursery isn't nearly as much fun when you're not there to chat to.'

'Oh, get away with you,' she chided, inwardly delighted

by the comment, although it was the last thing she should have been.

Fortunately, Jack let it drop as he escorted her and Sam to his car. They got the boys settled and drove the short distance to Tregorran House, where Lucy and Ben lived. The rest of the party had beaten them to it, so they decided to park in the lane to save blocking anyone in. Alison gasped as she got out of the car.

'I'd forgotten how gorgeous this place is. Just look at that view. It's stunning whichever way you look.'

She turned and drank it all in. The house had been built close to the cliff top and the view across the sea from the front garden was breathtaking. It had been a working farm originally, and the house was surrounded by fields. She could see cattle grazing in one of the fields close by—big Guernsey cows with red and white coats that gleamed in the sunshine. In another field the first spring lambs were frolicking around their mothers on spindly little legs.

'I wish I could afford a house like this,' she said wistfully. 'It's the perfect place to raise a child, isn't it?'

'It is.'

Alison frowned when she heard the roughness in Jack's voice. 'You're not still fretting about Freddie, are you? He's fine, Jack. Honestly, he is.' She laid her hand on his arm, wanting in some small way to offer him her support. She couldn't bear to think that he was worrying himself to death when there was no need.

'I'm sure you're right. Ignore me. I'm just a worry-wart.' He gave her a quick smile before he moved away. Alison sighed softly, wondering if she'd overstepped the mark. It really wasn't her place to keep on offering him advice, was it?

She helped Sam out of the car and took him inside. They used the back door, which led straight into the kitchen. Lucy welcomed them with glasses of champagne for the adults and fruit juice for the children. Alison thanked her, then went through to the sitting room, where most of the guests had congregated close to the buffet table. She let Sam choose what he wanted to eat and got him settled on a stool in the corner out of everyone's way, then went back to fill a plate for herself.

Jack was talking to his father and a strikingly attractive auburn-haired woman whom Alison had never seen before. It was obvious from their body language that she and Jack knew one another, and Alison couldn't help wondering who she was. An old flame of Jack's perhaps? Or a new conquest?

She took a sip of her champagne, but it tasted as flat as tap water all of a sudden. Jack had claimed that he wasn't in the market for a relationship last weekend, but maybe he hadn't been entirely truthful. He might not be interested in having a relationship with *her*, but he didn't appear to have any such reservations when it came to other women.

Pain lanced through her as she turned so that she couldn't see them. She had been right to steer clear of Jack. He was nothing but trouble.

Jack could barely contain his relief when he spotted Alex Ross talking to his father. He desperately needed to get back on track after what had happened outside, and he couldn't think of a better way of doing it than by talking to Alex and Nick. Did Alison have any idea what she did to him? he wondered as he led Freddie across the room. He sincerely hoped not. If she had even the faintest inkling of what he'd been thinking just now, she probably wouldn't speak to him again!

Jack's teeth snapped together when he felt desire surge through him once more. The sight of Alison standing in the sunlight with her blonde hair blowing gently in the breeze was one he was going to have the devil of a job to shift. What made it all the more scary was that she hadn't been trying to seduce him. She'd simply been admiring the view, oblivious to the fact that he'd been admiring *her*. It was her total lack of artifice that affected him so much. While other women he'd met had capitalised on their looks, she seemed genuinely unaware of her own beauty.

'Jack! I had no idea you were going to be here today until I saw you in church. Why didn't you tell me that you and Ben are related by marriage?'

Jack drummed up a smile as Alex greeted him in her usual forthright manner. 'It never cropped up.' He nodded to Nick. 'It was a lovely service, wasn't it, Dad?'

'It was,' Nick agreed, smiling at Freddie. 'And how are you today, Freddie? Have you been a good boy?'

Jack was amazed when Freddie nodded, and even more amazed when his father delved into his pocket and came up with a bag of chocolate buttons. He shook his head when his son eagerly accepted them. 'I never thought I'd see the day when you handed out sweets. It was Mum who always gave us any treats.'

Nick shrugged. 'It's a granddad's privilege to spoil his grandchildren.'

'Really?' Jack laughed. 'I'd better warn Lucy to be on the lookout for such subversive behaviour when Annabel gets a bit older.'

Alex smiled. 'I think it's lovely that you all live so close to each other. It must be a huge relief to you especially, Jack, having your family around to help you with Freddie.'

'It is. It's the reason I came back to Penhally Bay. Knowing that I could ask Lucy for help if I came unstuck was a big incentive.'

'And not just Lucy,' Alex said, glancing pointedly at Nick.

'No, of course not.' Jack took a deep breath, knowing this was the moment he'd been working up to. 'Having Dad around is a great help as well. I really value his support.'

Nick didn't say anything, so Jack couldn't tell how he felt about the comment. He was glad that he'd made it, though, because it was time he tried to build some bridges between them. The conversation moved on to more general topics after that, and Jack was surprised when Alex told them that she had been looking at sites to build a new clinic in the area. It appeared that she had been approached by a consortium that was keen to break into the lucrative cosmetic surgery market, and Rock had been chosen as a possible location.

Nick shook his head. 'It's not private health care we need here, but more investment in local services. St Piran Hospital struggles to balance its books year after year and it needs extra funding.'

'I'm sure that's true,' Alex said calmly. 'However, it's a completely separate issue. The clinic would offer a range of services not available on the NHS.'

'Tummy tucks and breast enlargements, you mean?' Nick said scornfully.

'Along with a host of other treatments, yes.' Alex shrugged. 'There's a huge demand nowadays because people want to look their best.'

'Even though they're placing themselves at risk by undergoing what is effectively major surgery.'

Jack could tell that his father was growing increasingly irate and hurriedly stepped in. 'So long as people are made aware of the risks, they can make an informed decision.'

'So you're in favour of this clinic, are you?' Nick snapped.

'I'm not against it. It's a question of personal choice, in my view,' Jack said.

'And no doubt you'll be happy to work in the place if it does get off the ground.' Nick smiled tightly. 'Why am I not surprised? It's only what I would have expected.'

Jack could feel his temper soar, but he didn't retaliate. 'You might not know me as well as you think, Dad. Now, if you'll both excuse me, I'll get Freddie something to eat.'

He led Freddie away, wondering why he had bothered to try to make his peace with his father when Nick seemed determined to think the worst of him. Lucy caught up with him at the buffet and shook her head.

'Don't tell me that you and Dad have had another argument.'

'I didn't argue. There's no point. Dad thinks he knows everything about me so why should I bother trying to change his mind?'

'He misses Mum and that's why he's so testy,' Lucy said softly.

'We *all* miss Mum, but we have to try and carry on as she would expect us to do,' Jack said shortly.

'I know that, but it's different for Dad. He's lost the woman he loved and expected to spend his life with.' Lucy glanced over at Ben, who was holding baby Annabel, and shivered. 'I can't imagine how awful it would be if anything happened to Ben. I don't even want to try.'

'Nothing is going to happen to Ben,' Jack said firmly, giving her a hug. The last thing he wanted to do was to spoil this special day for her. 'Anyway, if you nag Ben as much as you nag me then he will make sure he takes good care of himself just to stop you giving him earache!'

'Pig!'

She playfully punched him on the shoulder, then went to reclaim her daughter. Jack helped Freddie to some mini-sausages, relieved that Lucy's day hadn't been ruined by his remarks. He glanced up when someone jogged his elbow and found himself staring straight into Alison's eyes, and all of a sudden he understood exactly how Lucy felt. He didn't know what he would do if anything happened to Alison. He couldn't bear to think about it either.

His heart began to race as the full impact of that thought hit him. It might not be the right time for him or for Alison but it was happening anyway. He was falling in love with her and there wasn't a thing he could do about it.

CHAPTER TWELVE

THE party broke up just before five o'clock. Alison found Sam, who was playing in the kitchen with Freddie, and explained that it was time to go home. Both boys accompanied her as she went to say goodbye to Lucy and Ben.

'Thank you so much for inviting us. It's been really lovely.'

'It's you who deserves the thanks,' Lucy replied, giving her a hug. 'I'm really grateful to you for stepping in like that and taking charge of Freddie.'

'It was nothing,' Alison assured her. She ran a gentle hand over Freddie's dark curls, unaware how revealing her expression was. 'Jack needs all the help he can get at the moment, doesn't he?'

'He certainly does,' Lucy replied, nudging Ben in the ribs. 'Go and find Jack, darling. I'm sure he'd like to say goodbye to Alison.'

'Oh, um, right you are,' Ben agreed, giving Lucy a funny look as he hurried away.

'There's really no need to bother Jack,' Alison said quickly.

'Rubbish!' Lucy said robustly. 'If I know my brother, he'll be most upset if I let you leave without saying goodbye. Aha, here he is now. See, I was right.'

'I…um…yes.' Alison said softly, wishing the floor would

open up and swallow her. Jack could have spent any amount of time with her that afternoon if he'd wanted to. The fact that he'd made a point of avoiding her after she'd bumped into him at the buffet table merely proved he hadn't been interested. She was mortified to think that he might believe she was responsible for Ben dragging him away from his friends.

'Lucy insisted I should say goodbye to you,' she said quickly.

'And quite right, too.' Jack treated her to one of his most dazzling smiles. It left her feeling cold, because there wasn't a scrap of genuine emotion in it.

'Thank you again for looking after Freddie,' he continued, unaware that her heart was aching so hard she could hardly stand the pain. There was no sign of the warmth she'd seen in his eyes earlier in the day and she couldn't help wondering what had changed. Was it the fact that there was someone else he wanted to charm more than her?

As though on cue, the woman Jack had been speaking to earlier suddenly appeared. She came over to them, holding out her hand as she smiled at Lucy. 'Thank you so much for inviting me join you on such a special day.'

'Thank you for coming,' Lucy replied politely. She turned to Alison. 'Did you two get a chance to meet? There were so many people here that I didn't get round to making all the introductions. Alison, this is Alex Ross—Jack's new boss, for her sins!'

Everyone laughed. Alison did her best to join in, even though the situation seemed to be going from bad to worse. She'd had no idea the woman was Jack's boss, and the thought of them working together on a daily basis was very difficult to handle. Putting out her hand, she forced herself to smile at Alex Ross.

'It's nice to meet you. I'm Alison Myers, one of the practice nurses.'

'Delighted to meet you, Alison.'

Alex shook her hand, then said her goodbyes and left, pausing on the way out to have a final word with Jack. Alison could feel her insides churning as she watched them. What were they discussing? she wondered. The welfare of one of their patients, or when they would meet again?

Jealousy clawed at her insides, and she caught hold of Sam's hand and quickly led him out of the door. It was only when she realised that Freddie had followed them that she stopped. Crouching down, she gave the little boy a hug.

'Sam and I have to go home now, sweetheart. You must stay here with your daddy.'

Freddie's lower lip wobbled as he clutched hold of her coat sleeve, and she sighed. She didn't want to upset him, but she desperately wanted to go home.

'You seem to have made a big impression on him.'

She looked up when Jack came hurrying over to them, and saw the smile that still lingered around his mouth. It was a world away from the one he had treated her to, and the thought that Alex Ross had been the recipient of it stung.

'I don't know about that,' she said crisply, standing up. 'However, I'm afraid Sam and I really have to go now.'

'I'll give you a lift,' Jack said immediately. He swept Freddie into his arms, not giving her time to explain that she didn't want a lift as he turned to his sister and brother-in-law. 'It's been really great today. Freddie and I have both enjoyed it—haven't we, Freddie?'

'We've enjoyed having you here,' Lucy said, kissing her nephew on the cheek.

Alison didn't utter a word as they set off down the drive. Jack had just ridden roughshod over her wishes as though he didn't give a damn how she felt. She could feel anger bubbling inside her by the time they reached his car. She strapped Sam in, then opened the passenger door and climbed inside, still without uttering a word. Jack got in beside her, one dark brow rising as he caught sight of her thunderous expression.

'What's wrong?'

'You know what's wrong,' she retorted, dragging her seat belt across her. She ground her teeth when the mechanism locked before she could fasten it. No amount of pulling would release it either. When Jack leant over and took the buckle from her hands and fastened it in place, she could have screamed.

He didn't say a word as he started the engine and his silence was the most effective cure for her fit of pique. Alison felt so ashamed of herself that she could have wept. What on earth was she thinking about by behaving that way? It was hardly a good example for the children, was it?

By the time they reached her house, she felt so wretched that all she wanted to do was run inside and hide. She climbed out of the car, shaking her head when Jack went to get out as well.

'You stay there. I can manage.'

She lifted Sam out of the back, said goodbye to Freddie, then shut the door. Jack zoomed down the window and leant across the passenger seat.

'If I've done something to upset you, Alison, I'm sorry.'

'You haven't.'

One last strained smile and she was free to go. She didn't glance back as she ushered Sam up the path and into the house. She took off his coat and gave him a drink of milk, determined that she wasn't going to fall apart in front of him. However, when he went into the sitting room to play with his toys, she couldn't hold on any longer.

She sank down on a chair as tears filled her eyes. She

wasn't used to feeling like this. She had never been jealous when she'd been married to Gareth. Not even when she had found out that he'd been having an affair. Oh, she'd been hurt and angry, but it had been nothing compared to how she'd felt she'd seen Jack and Alex together. Was this what true love felt like? The sort of love she'd read about in books? She had no idea, but the thought scared her. She didn't want to fall in love with Jack if she ended up getting hurt.

Jack couldn't settle. He kept thinking about what had happened when he had dropped Alison off at her house. He knew that she'd been angry and upset but he had no idea why. He paced the sitting-room floor after Freddie had gone to bed, trying to work out what he had done, but it was impossible to make sense of it. All he knew was that he wouldn't be able to rest until he had sorted everything out.

He went out to the hall and picked up the phone, then paused. Bearing in mind what had happened at the christening party, was it right to ask his father to babysit for him? However, if he didn't ask Nick then he might never get the chance to clear up this misunderstanding. He groaned. Talk about being caught on the horns of a dilemma! Either he phoned his father and risked a rebuff, or he risked never resolving this issue with Alison. Both prospects were highly unappealing, but he knew which one was worse.

It took a half dozen rings before Nick answered the phone, and Jack had reached desperation point by then, so he didn't waste any time on non-essentials. 'Dad, it's me. Look, I hate to ask you after the way we parted earlier on today, but I desperately need a favour. Will you babysit for me?'

Half an hour later he was on his way to Alison's house. Nick had agreed immediately to look after Freddie for him and, even more surprisingly, he hadn't asked Jack where he was going either. Jack wasn't sure what he would have said if his father had questioned him. He couldn't have lied to him, neither could he have told him the truth. All he could do was thank his stars that for once Nick had given him the benefit of the doubt. He grimaced as he pulled up outside Alison's house. He had a feeling that he was going to need every scrap of luck he could get if he hoped to persuade her to open up to him.

He walked up the path, then took a deep breath before he knocked on the front door. The first few seconds were crucial if he hoped to persuade her to let him in. He needed to strike the right note—calm and friendly, not too pushy, and definitely not desperate. He hurriedly pinned a smile to his face when the door opened.

'Hi! I thought I'd pop round and see how you were.'

'I'm fine,' she said shortly. 'Why shouldn't I be?'

'Oh, no reason. You just appeared a bit uptight when I dropped you off before.'

Her brows rose. 'Uptight? Whatever gave you that idea?'

'It was just a feeling I had…' He tailed off, very much afraid that he had blown it. He hadn't even got inside the house and already he was floundering.

'A feeling? I see. Well, I can assure you that you were mistaken. I was fine then and I'm fine now, thank you, Jack.'

'That's all right, then.' He dredged up another smile, although the brightness had faded from this one. He'd been a fool to come, and a double fool to imagine that Alison cared a jot about him. He swung round, not wanting her to know how stupid he felt. 'I'm sorry I bothered you.'

'Jack, wait. Don't go.'

He'd got to the end of the path before she spoke, and even then he wasn't sure if he'd actually heard her. He paused, undecided whether he should turn round and check. If it was his imagination playing tricks, he'd look even more foolish…

And if it wasn't, he would have lost his one and only chance to sort this out with her.

He swung round and felt his heart start to race when he saw the torment on her face. It took him just a couple of strides to reach the door, but it felt as though he'd travelled to the moon and back by the time he got there. Alison stared at him for a moment and he could tell that she was trying to decide what to do. He could barely contain his delight when she stepped back.

'You'd better come in.'

Jack followed her inside and made it safely along the hall, even though his legs felt as though they were filled with jelly. She stopped in the middle of the sitting room and turned to him, and he could see the fear in her eyes. He knew that if he'd been stronger he would have turned around and left, only he wasn't strong enough to leave her now.

One step brought him within touching distance, so he touched her—just one finger skimming across the back of her wrist. Their skin made the minimal amount of contact, yet he sucked in his breath when he felt a heat so intense he could barely stand it sear his veins.

Another step took him closer still, close enough to feel the heat that was emanating from her in waves, and he shuddered, unable to pretend that it didn't affect him in any way. She stared back at him with bewilderment on her face.

'I never knew it could feel like this.'

'Neither did I,' he ground out as he took the final step, the one that brought his body up hard against hers. Flames licked along his fingers as they closed around her arms, scorched his chest as he drew her to him and held her so that he could feel her heart beating wildly against him. When he bent his head and pressed his mouth to the hollow of her throat, he was completely consumed by the fire.

'Jack...'

Her voice was the softest whisper as she murmured his name, but it fanned the flames of his desire. He kissed her again, then let his tongue trace the delicate hollow between her neck and her collar-bone, taste the softness of her flesh, and groaned. Kissing her aroused so many emotions inside him, ones he had never experienced in his entire life.

He raised his head and looked deep into her eyes, knowing that she would see how much he wanted her. He refused to pretend that his need was less than it was, even if it was too much for her to accept. He wanted her in every way a man could want a woman, and she needed to understand that.

Colour bloomed in her face, rushed down her throat, and she trembled, but she didn't look away. She met his gaze proudly, almost defiantly, and Jack could have wept because he understood how much it must have cost her.

Pulling her back into his arms, he rained kisses on her hair, her forehead, the delicate slope of her nose. By the time he reached her mouth they were both trembling, both desperate to sate their hunger. When his mouth finally found hers, he heard her sigh and sighed as well, because it was such a relief to know that he was welcome, wanted; that he no longer scared her.

He kissed her long and hungrily as his passion soared until it reached previously undiscovered heights. The taste of her mouth, the whisper of her breath, the feel of her in his arms was even more potent than he had imagined. He could feel his body reacting to her closeness and shifted slightly, afraid that he was going too fast for her, but she put her arms around him and pressed herself against him, and it was like setting light to touch paper.

He tore his mouth away from hers. When he'd made love with a woman in the past he had deliberately held part of himself back, but he couldn't do that now and didn't want to. Not with Alison. If they made love he would give her his all, and he wanted her to welcome him without any reservations.

'I want to make love to you, but if it isn't what you want too, then say so.' His voice sounded ragged with passion, but he didn't care. He took her face between his hands, his heart overflowing with tenderness as he looked into her eyes. 'I would never do anything to hurt you, sweetheart. I swear.'

'I know you wouldn't.' Reaching up, she kissed him on the mouth, her lips parting so that her tongue could mesh with his, and Jack shuddered. He had his answer now—an answer he had hardly dared to hope he would get.

He gathered her to him and kissed her softly, but with a passion that left them both trembling when he drew back. Alison held out her hand, looking so beautiful as she stood there with her lips all rosy from his kisses that he couldn't speak. He took her hand and let her lead him from the room and up the stairs, his mind in a daze, his body in heaven. When she opened her bedroom door and turned to him, he lifted her into his arms and carried her to the bed. They didn't need words when they had this. Didn't need anything except each other.

CHAPTER THIRTEEN

ALISON closed her eyes as Jack laid her on the bed. She wanted to savour this moment, store it away for ever and always. She felt the mattress lift as he stood up, then heard a click as he turned on the lamp. Only then did she open her eyes, and she felt her heart melt when she found him staring down at her with such tenderness on his face. In that second she realised that what was happening meant as much to him as it did to her. Jack couldn't look at her that way if he didn't care.

The thought chased away any doubts she might have had. Holding out her hand, she smiled at him, faintly shocked yet secretly delighted by her own boldness. She had never initiated sex before, but she was going to take the lead now.

'Why don't you come and keep me company? It's rather lonely in this great big bed.'

Jack chuckled as he sat down on the edge of the mattress. 'I would hate you to be lonely.' He kissed her on the mouth, then drew back and looked at her. 'Feeling better now?'

'A bit.' Alison smiled up at him, loving the way the lamplight played across his face, highlighting his clean-cut features and the richness of his dark hair.

'Only a bit?' His brows arched. 'So that means you still feel a bit lonesome, does it?'

'Hmm. But I'm sure we can do something to remedy that.'

Alison let her hand glide up his arm, her fingers sliding beneath the sleeve of his jacket, and heard him suck in his breath. His response was so encouraging that it made her bolder still, her other hand moving to his chest and skimming over the hard pectoral muscles. He was wearing the shirt he'd worn to the christening—soft blue cotton that flowed beneath her palm. She could feel the heat of his skin seeping through the fabric, and shivered as she imagined how it would feel to touch him without anything in the way.

Jack captured her hand and raised it to his lips, pressing a lingering kiss to the centre of her palm. 'If it's any consolation, I don't feel the least bit lonely. In fact, I can't remember when I ever felt this content.'

'Good.' Alison smiled up at him, deeply touched by the admission. To know that she was enough for Jack was more than she could have hoped for. When he released her hand, she placed it back on his chest, memorising his body by touch as well as by sight. She wanted to *soak* herself in him, absorb everything that made him the man he was.

Jack let her explore for a few more minutes, then shook his head. 'If we carry on this way, I'll be fit for nothing. And then we'll both end up feeling extremely lonely *and* frustrated.'

Alison blushed, and he laughed as he dropped a kiss on the tip of her nose. 'I love it when you blush like that. I don't think I've met anyone who's so wonderfully innocent.'

'I'm not a complete innocent,' she protested, but he shushed her with a finger on her lips.

'Yes, you are, and it's a compliment, too. I find your lack of artifice a real turn-on.'

He kissed her again, proving to her in the most effective way possible that he was telling her the truth. Alison had always believed that her lack of experience had been a hindrance in the past, but suddenly it felt like a blessing rather than something to be ashamed of. She kissed him back as passion surged between them, long, drugging kisses that filled her with joy. It was only when he started to unbutton her blouse that the first doubts crept in and she shivered.

It had been a long time since a man had seen her naked, and she was suddenly afraid that Jack wouldn't like what he saw. Gareth had been scathing about her figure after she'd had Sam; he'd even told her that it had been one of the reasons why he'd had an affair. She was terrified that Jack would feel the same way when he saw her undressed. After all, her breasts weren't as firm as they'd been, and she had a couple of stretch marks on her hips from carrying Sam. What if Jack was repulsed by the sight of her? What would she do then...?

'It's OK, sweetheart. If you want me to stop, you only have to say so.'

The understanding in Jack's voice brought a rush of tears to her eyes and he gathered her close, murmuring to her as he stroked her hair. 'Shush, now. It's all right. There's no need to cry. I didn't mean to scare you.'

'It isn't you,' she mumbled through a mouthful of pale blue cotton.

'Then what is it?' He set her away from him, his gaze very gentle as he looked at her in concern.

'It's me. I...I'm afraid you'll think that I...I'm ugly.'

'Ugly?' he repeated, and she lowered her head because she couldn't bear to look at him while she explained.

'I've had a baby, and I'm not...well, I don't look the same as I did before I was pregnant,' she whispered.

'And you think I won't like what I see?'

'Yes. My ex-husband told me that was why he had an affair...' She tailed off, then dredged up the very last drop of her courage. She needed to be completely honest with

Jack about this. 'He said he couldn't bear to make love to me after I'd had Sam.'

Jack swore loudly, then hurriedly apologised. 'I'm sorry. That's not the kind of language I would normally use around you.' He tilted her chin and made her look at him. 'I don't know exactly what your ex said to you, and I don't want to know either. However, take it from me that it was a pack of lies. No man stops loving a woman because her body has changed. It doesn't work like that.'

Tears spilled from her eyes and trickled down her cheeks. 'But you haven't seen what I look like yet.'

'No, and that's something I intend to rectify immediately.'

He kissed her softly, then laid her down on the pillows and carried on unfastening her blouse, punctuating the process with kisses along the way. When he came to the final button, he paused to smile at her. 'It's going to be wonderful, Alison. *You* are wonderful.'

Alison wanted to believe him, but she was holding her breath as he parted the blouse and slid it off her shoulders. Her bra came next, then her skirt and her panties, and she was naked. She squeezed her eyes tight shut because she couldn't bear to watch his face.

'You are *so* beautiful.'

The awe in his voice brought her eyes open and she stared at him in amazement. 'Beautiful?'

'Yes.' He couldn't seem to drag his gaze away from her. His hands were shaking as he cupped her breasts and allowed their weight to settle in his palms. 'You look like a woman should look—all soft curves and even softer skin—'

He broke off and gulped, raising his head so that she saw the desire that had tightened the bones of his face, and every single horrible thing Gareth had said to her was erased from her mind with one single stroke. Jack couldn't look at her this way if he didn't want her!

She sat up and put her arms around his neck, held him to her and gloried in the wonder of being able to do such a thing. When he started to unfasten his shirt she helped him, laughing when he managed to rip off a couple of the buttons in his haste.

'Shall I do it for you?' she offered with a teasing smile.

Jack sat as still as statue while she undid the rest of the buttons. He didn't move a muscle when she undid his cufflinks either. However, when she reached for the buckle on his belt, he stopped her.

'I think I'd better do the rest.'

He kissed her quickly, then stood up and stripped off his trousers and his underwear, leaving her in little doubt as to why he'd felt it necessary to take over the task. Alison felt heat pool low in her belly as he came and lay down beside her. She could feel his erection pressing against her as he drew her into the cradle of his hips, feel her own response to his nearness, and it stunned her that she should be so aroused. She had never wanted any man as much as she wanted Jack at that moment.

He kissed her long and lingeringly, then stroked her breasts until her nipples peaked. Bending his head, he drew first one nipple and then the other into his mouth and suckled her until she could barely think because of the sensations that were pouring through her. When he laid her back against the pillows again and let his mouth glide down her body, stopping to kiss her en route, she shifted restlessly, unable to satisfy the hunger that was building inside her.

His lips stopped on her belly, just above the nest of curls at the junction of her thighs, while his fingers explored the very source of her heat and she cried out. She wasn't sure what was happening to her because she'd never felt this way before. All she could think about was the tension that was building inside her and her desperate need for relief.

Jack held her close as she climaxed, feeling his heart pounding from the effort it had cost him to hold onto his control. He hadn't expected her to be so sweetly responsive to his touch, so it felt like a gift to know that he could please her like this. He held her until she stopped trembling, then smiled into her eyes, knowing at that moment how much he loved her. It had to be love, of course—real love, not just sexual attraction. It couldn't be anything less when he felt this way—all fired up, yet ready to forfeit his own pleasure to ensure hers. His gaze skimmed over her flushed face, drinking in every single emotion that was etched on it: passion, yes; satisfaction, that was a given after the way she had responded to him; shock... Shock?

He swallowed hard to ease the knot of tension that suddenly tightened his throat. The only reason he could think of to explain why Alison appeared so shocked was impossible to accept. Surely it couldn't have been the first time that she'd had an orgasm?

His heart was pounding as he pulled her back into his arms. He longed to ask her if his suspicions were correct, but it wasn't the right time to ask her now. Her confidence had obviously taken a battering during her marriage, and what she needed most of all was a chance to regain her self-esteem. His heart overflowed with love at the thought, because he intended to do everything he could to help her!

He kissed her hungrily, using every skill he had to arouse her passion once more. It was sheer heaven to feel her tremble in his arms and have her cling to him. Even though he had gone way beyond the normal limits of his control he held back, wanting to be sure that she would gain as much from their union as he did, and she did. The last thing Jack heard before the world went spinning out of control was her crying out his name, and it was the sweetest, the most precious sound he had ever heard.

Daylight crept around the edges of the curtains and Alison woke up. For a moment she couldn't understand why she felt so different that morning. Then all of a sudden everything came flooding back—her and Jack, and what had happened in her bed.

Rolling onto her side, she studied his face. He looked much softer when he was asleep, younger too, and her heart welled with tenderness when she realised it. Reaching out, she traced the elegant curve of his brows with the tip of her finger, enjoying the silky feel of the dark hair against her skin. His nose came next, and she couldn't resist letting her fingertip skate down its elegant length. The only problem was that when she reached the bottom her finger was hovering just above his mouth and that was even more tempting.

She drew the tip of her finger lightly across his lips, and gasped when she felt tingles of sensation shoot through the palm of her hand. Although she was the one doing the caressing rather than being caressed, the effect was just as stimulating. She traced a path around his lips until she'd completed a full circuit of his mouth. Even then she wasn't satisfied, so she went back for a second trip—across his Cupid's bow, into one curling corner, round to the bottom, along to the middle...

She jumped when his lips suddenly parted and he drew her finger into his mouth. Her eyes flew to his and she felt heat invade her when she realised he was watching her. Holding her gaze, he sucked the tip of her finger, then let his mouth graze across her palm until it came to her wrist, to the very spot where her pulse was beating so wildly, and licked it.

Alison closed her eyes as a wave of passion gripped her. She couldn't believe that such a seemingly simple action could arouse her this way. When Jack rolled her over onto her back and let his mouth explore the rest of her body she didn't protest. Now that she knew how desire felt, she wanted to enjoy it again and again, wanted Jack to show her how wonderful it felt to be loved.

They made love, and it was just as breathtaking that morning as it had been the night before. Alison clung to him as the world seemed to shudder to a stop, felt him cling to her and knew he felt the same way. They had aroused one another's passion and satisfied it too, and it was the most wonderful feeling to know that she could give Jack what he needed. It had restored her belief in herself as a woman. When he drew her into his arms after everything had stopped spinning, she knew that she had to tell him that. It would be her gift to him, the best way she knew to thank him.

'I've never felt like this before,' she whispered. 'I wasn't even sure if I could feel this way. You've shown me how it feels to be a real woman.'

'Thank you,' he said just as quietly, although she could tell how moved he was. He kissed her on the mouth, then looked into her eyes. 'This has been very special for me, too. I've never felt this way about anyone before.'

It was so wonderful to hear him say that that she couldn't speak, and he kissed her again. They would have continued kissing, too, if the sound of footsteps on the landing hadn't warned her that Sam was awake. Although she wasn't ashamed of what she'd done, she didn't want Sam walking in on them and wondering what was going on.

'Sam's awake,' she explained, pushing back the bedclothes. She reached for her robe and pulled it on. 'I'd better go and see to him.'

'And I'd better go home and check that Freddie's all right.'

Jack got up and reached for his clothes, which were lying in a heap on the floor. He grimaced as he picked up his shirt. 'I'd better come up with a good story for Dad to explain the state of my clothes, too.'

Alison paused on her way to the door. 'Are you going to tell him where you've been?'

'I don't think so.' He finished buttoning his shirt and tucked it into his trousers. 'I think it's best if we keep quiet about what's happened. We don't want everyone gossiping about us, do we?'

'Of course not,' she said quickly, wondering why she felt so uneasy all of a sudden. She knew how quickly rumours could spread throughout the town, and she would hate to think that people were talking about them. However, as she left the bedroom she couldn't help wondering if Jack was more concerned about the people he worked with finding out, and one person in particular. How would Alex Ross feel if she discovered that Jack had spent the night with her?

The thought nagged away at her while she was seeing to Sam. Jack managed to slip away while she was getting the little boy dressed, so at least she didn't have to explain what he'd been doing there at that time of the day. She'd given no thought to the implications of what had happened last night, but there was no way that she would allow Sam to be adversely affected by it. If she and Jack continued seeing each other, they would have to be discreet.

Fear clutched her heart, because it really was a question of *if*, wasn't it? Jack hadn't arranged to see her again, and there was no guarantee that he would. One night and one morning didn't constitute a commitment on either side. This might be the beginning and the end of their relationship.

As the day wore on, Jack's doubts about what had happened gathered pace. Although he didn't deny that it had been the most moving experience of his life, he knew in his heart that he should never have allowed it to happen. At the present moment he had so much else going on in his life that he didn't have time for a relationship, at least not the sort of relationship he wanted with Alison.

It had been so simple in the past. He'd separated his life into two separate compartments—his career and his social life—and he had kept them strictly apart. That was why he had never shared his home with a woman or involved her in his working life in any way, shape or form. However, he couldn't do that with Alison.

He wanted her to be involved in every aspect of his life, and that was bound to have repercussions not only for him, but for Freddie. Although Freddie seemed to like her, it was too soon to introduce her into his son's life on a permanent basis. Freddie was only just getting used to *him* and it would confuse him if the dynamics of their relationship had to change. Bluntly, Freddie might not want to share him with someone else. The thought weighed heavily on him as he worked.

Becca had been discharged at the weekend, and Ryan had an appointment with the consultant in London the following day. Jack popped in to see him, to check that he understood what was going to happen.

'So you're quite happy with the arrangements? There's an ambulance booked to take you up to London. I'm not sure how long you'll be there—that will be up to the consultant to decide once he's seen you,' he explained. 'Are your parents going with you?'

Ryan shook his head. 'Mum can't get the time off work and Dad's no use. He'll only start drinking and make a scene, so it's best if he stays away.'

Jack sighed. 'That means you'll have nobody around to visit you.'

'Oh, it's OK. Becca has promised to come and see me every day.' Ryan grinned at him and Jack laughed.

'I see.' He shook the boy's hand. 'Good luck, then. Not that you'll need it. Take it from me that you're getting the very best possible care.'

He was still smiling as he left the ward. Alex was just coming in and she stopped to speak to him.

'You're looking a lot happier than you did this morning. Has something cheered you up?'

'I've just been speaking to Ryan Lovelace,' Jack explained, somewhat surprised by the comment because he hadn't realised he was so transparent. He hurried on, not wanting to dwell on the thought. 'He's arranged for Becca to visit him while he's in London.'

'I see. Do I detect a hint of romance in the air?'

'I think the answer to that is watch this space!'

Alex laughed as she carried on into the ward. Jack went to the office and made sure that Ryan's notes were up to date. He had just finished and was thinking about going home when there was a call from A and E. Jack responded, and decided that the patient needed to go straight to Theatre. The young man had suffered extensive tissue damage after his motorbike had skidded. He hadn't been wearing protective clothing and a large area of skin and flesh had been sheared away from his right thigh.

Jack called Theatre and arranged for everything to be set up in readiness, then phoned Lucy and asked her if she would collect Freddie from the nursery. Although he felt bad about abandoning his son again after last night, he didn't have a choice. Still, Freddie had been fine when he'd got home that morning. He'd obviously enjoyed having his grandfather there to spoil him, so Jack wasn't too worried. The sooner Freddie got used to the people who loved him, the better it would be for him.

Freddie would probably get used to Alison, too, a small voice whispered inside his head, but Jack blanked it out. Probably wasn't good enough—not for Freddie and not for Alison. Until he was sure that neither of them would get hurt, he couldn't do anything about the current situation. He intended to protect his son *and* protect the woman he loved.

CHAPTER FOURTEEN

A week passed and Alison didn't hear a word from Jack. Every time the phone rang or someone knocked on the door, she kept thinking it would be him, but it never was. She even went back to taking Sam to the nursery at the usual time, but somehow she always seemed to miss Jack. She could only conclude that he was avoiding her, and it hurt. It seemed that sleeping together hadn't been as wonderful an experience for him as he had claimed.

She tried to deal with her heartache by keeping busy. It wasn't difficult because they were inundated at the surgery. An outbreak of some sort of particularly nasty stomach bug kept the phones ringing almost non-stop. Morning and afternoon surgeries were full to overflowing, and in the end Nick decided that anyone who was complaining of gastric problems should be told to stay at home. They would receive a home visit rather than run the risk of spreading the bug any further.

The decision had a knock-on effect for everyone. With all the doctors doing house calls each day, inevitably afternoon surgeries started late. Alison had to make arrangements for Sam to stay with the childminder for an extra hour each day, and that seemed to upset his routine, so he started playing up. After a week of temper tantrums, she was longing for the time when life would get back to normal. Dealing with a fretful three-year-old *and* an aching heart was taxing her to the limit.

The day of Maggie's hen night arrived, but Alison decided to give it a miss. Sam was still being difficult, and she didn't want to leave him with a babysitter, plus she didn't feel in the mood for partying. Gemma tried to change her mind but she stuck to her decision. She'd much prefer a quiet night at home.

The day flew past, although it wasn't as busy as it had been. The bug was running its course, and there were far fewer phone calls and home visits. Consequently, it was only a little after her normal time when she collected Sam, and to her delight he seemed more like his usual sunny self. They had tea, then played a game before bedtime. Alison read him his favourite story and tucked him in, sighing in relief when he immediately closed his eyes. It seemed the crisis was over in more ways than one. If only her problems with Jack could be resolved so satisfactorily she would feel so much better. Should she phone him and ask him to call round? Or should she leave him to get in touch with her—if he ever did?

She spent ages thinking about it, but couldn't make up her mind. In the end she went to bed with the problem unresolved, and woke up the following morning still worrying about it. Part of her wanted to make the first move, but another part of her was terrified of inviting a rebuff.

Saturday was another glorious day, so she decided to forgo the usual household chores and take Sam out. Once again, she headed to Rock, trying not to think about what had happened the last time she'd been there. She intended to enjoy this day with Sam and not keep thinking about Jack all the time.

She made for a sheltered stretch of the bay that overlooked the Camel estuary. There were quite a few people already there when she and Sam arrived, mainly family groups with small children who were playing in the sand. Alison chose a spot close to the water's edge and helped Sam take off his shoes and socks so he could paddle. She had a spare set of clothes in the car so it didn't matter if he got wet. As long as he was having fun, that was the main thing.

They'd been there about an hour when she spotted two familiar figures walking along the beach. Her heart leapt into her throat when she recognised Jack and Freddie. Had Jack guessed that she would be here and come looking for her? she wondered as she scrambled to her feet. All of a sudden the doubts that had plagued her all week long seemed so stupid that she laughed out loud. The only reason Jack hadn't been in touch with her was because he'd been too busy!

She lifted her hand to wave to him, then suddenly realised that he and Freddie weren't on their own. There was a woman with them, the tall woman with auburn hair she remembered from the christening. Alison felt her stomach roll with sickness as she saw Jack turn and reply to something Alex Ross had said to him. The tilt of his head and the smile that played around his mouth were all too familiar. He was looking at Alex the same way he had looked at her the other night, and she couldn't bear it. She simply couldn't bear it!

It was far too late by then for her to run away and hide. She had to stand there and wait as they approached. Her heart ached when she saw Jack's expression alter when he spotted her. She turned away, not wanting to witness his discomfort. It wasn't difficult to imagine how awkward he felt. He may have been happy enough to sleep with her, but she wasn't the sort of woman he would normally be interested in. That honour went to someone like Alex Ross, someone who was beautiful and sophisticated and worldly-wise. What would Jack want with a little nobody like her?

'Hi! I had no idea you'd be here,' he said quietly as he and Alex stopped. Freddie spotted Sam and immediately ran over to him. Alison shrugged as she watched the two children laughing together.

'It was just a spur-of-the-moment decision.'

'Oh. Right. I see.' A frown darkened his face for a second before he turned to Alex. 'You remember Alison, don't you?'

'Of course.'

Alex gave her a brief smile, but Alison could tell that she wasn't keen to prolong their meeting. She didn't blame her. If she'd been in Alex's shoes she wouldn't have wanted to share even a second of the time she had with Jack with some other woman. The thought brought a rush of tears to her eyes, and she quickly bent and gathered up Sam's shoes and socks.

'Actually, we were about to go home. It's been nice seeing you again, Alex,' she added politely.

'You, too,' Alex replied graciously. She carried on walking, but Jack hung back.

'You're not rushing off on our account, I hope.'

'No. You may find this hard to believe, Jack, but the world doesn't revolve around you.'

His jaw tightened. 'You're angry with me because I haven't been in touch. I don't blame you. I should have called you. I almost did—several times, in fact. I just didn't know what to say.'

'Really? I wouldn't have thought it would be that difficult. All you needed to say was that you'd made a mistake. How hard is that?'

'It isn't like that!' he denied hotly. 'You don't understand.'

'Oh, I think I do.' She stared back at him, bolstering up her anger to stave off the pain that was knifing through her. 'Making love to me the other night was fine, wasn't it, Jack? But you're not interested in making a commitment to me, are you?'

'No, I'm not,' he said bluntly. 'It's not the right time, for many reasons.'

'Not the right time, or not the right woman?'

'What do you mean?'

'I'm not your usual kind of woman, am I?'

'No, you're not.'

His voice was husky, and she shivered when she felt it stroke along her nerves, but she was too hurt and too angry to stop. She laughed harshly. 'That's what I thought. At least you have the decency to be honest with me. That's something in your favour.'

She tossed back her hair as the wind whipped it across her face, knowing that she had to end this for good. She mustn't allow herself to hope that Jack might come to love her one day. 'I'm not sure why you slept with me. Maybe it was a way to thank me for looking after Freddie for you, or maybe it was just an urge that needed satisfying—who knows? But it definitely won't happen again. Understand?'

'I understand. And you're right, Alison. It would be wrong for us to start something right now.' His expression was bleak. 'I need to focus on Freddie. I can't afford to take any chances where his happiness is concerned. He's been through too much already, and I won't risk upsetting his life any more.'

'And I feel the same way about Sam. I won't allow his life to be disrupted either.'

Jack nodded. 'Then it seems we're in complete agreement, doesn't it?'

'Yes.' Alison left it at that. There was nothing else to say anyway. Jack had made his position perfectly clear, although she wasn't stupid enough to think that he wouldn't change his mind if the circumstances were right.

The thought of what might make those circumstances conducive to him reconsidering his stance was very hard to deal with, and she shut it out of her mind. She didn't want to think about him and Alex, didn't want to imagine them making plans for their future together. It was none of her business what Jack did. It never had been.

She fetched Sam and dried his feet, then popped his shoes and socks back on. He begged her to let him stay and play with Freddie, but she was adamant that they had to go home. That set off another tantrum, but she didn't back down. Sam needed consistency in his life; he needed to know that when she said no she meant it.

If only she could make herself understand that concept when it came to Jack, she thought bitterly as she took Sam back to the car. She might have told Jack that she would never sleep with him again, but she knew how hard it would be to stick to that decision if the occasion ever arose. Where Jack was concerned she was as weak as a kitten, and it worried her to think that she might end up doing the one thing she would regret.

It made her wonder if she should leave Penhally Bay and remove herself from temptation, but where would she go? All her friends were here, as well as her job, and it would mean making a completely fresh start. It would also mean uprooting Sam, and that wouldn't be good for him either.

She sighed. It wasn't going to be easy, but she had to forget about Jack and get on with her life as she had been doing before he'd arrived. The problem was that now she'd had a taste of how wonderful life could be, it would be hard to settle for second best.

* * *

Jack knew that he'd made a complete and utter hash of things with Alison. He also knew there was nothing he could do at the moment to put things right. The thought weighed heavily on him, so that he found it hard to concentrate as Alex explained about the new clinic.

She had accepted an offer to be the clinic's director, and Jack knew that she was hoping to persuade him to be her second-in-command, which was why she had invited him to meet her at Rock that day. A site had been chosen and the plans were being drawn up, so it looked as though everything was going ahead. While he was flattered by her faith in his abilities, he couldn't make a decision while his life was in such a mess.

He made all the right noises, but he knew that Alex sensed he had reservations. She cut short their meeting, declining his offer of a cup of coffee with a quick shake of her head.

'Thanks, but I'll get off home. If there's anything I haven't covered, you know where I am.' She smiled at him. 'I won't take offence if you turn me down, Jack. You have to know that it's the right decision for you. I couldn't have imagined doing this type of work a few years ago either, but I've had enough of the NHS and all its problems. That's why I've accepted this job.'

'Thanks. I know it could be a great opportunity for me, but I'm just not sure if the time is right for me to make such a move.' He glanced at Freddie. 'I need to consider the impact it will have on Freddie's life, not just on my own.'

'If it's that which is bothering you then private medicine would suit you perfectly. No more callouts at the weekend or during the night, regular hours and a top salary.' She shrugged as she unlocked her car. 'However, I get the feeling it's more complicated than that, so take your time. The offer's there if you want it.'

Jack sighed as he watched her drive away. It would make

a lot of sense to take the job at the clinic, yet his gut feeling was to refuse it. He enjoyed what he did, and loved the fact that he could make such a difference to so many people's lives. He couldn't imagine giving it all up, even for the benefits of working in the private sector.

It was yet another uncertainty, and he could have done without it right now. He took Freddie home and settled down in the sitting room while they watched a cartoon together. For the first time ever Freddie climbed onto his knee, and Jack's heart overflowed with happiness. He desperately wanted to share the moment with Alison, but he couldn't phone her after what had happened that day. He had to let her get on with her life while he got on with his, and the thought took some of the shine away. He simply couldn't imagine living out the rest of his days without her.

As the end of the month drew near, Jack couldn't believe how much had happened in the weeks since he'd been back in Penhally Bay. Despite his heartache over Alison, he knew he'd made the right decision when he had moved back to Cornwall. Freddie was slowly adjusting to his new life. Although he still hadn't spoken, he seemed more content. He had fewer nightmares too, and even smiled at times. He seemed to enjoy nursery and he loved Lucy. He was also devoted to his grandfather, and Jack had to admit that he was surprised at how good Nick was with him. Nick genuinely seemed to care about Freddie, and that helped to smooth some of the rough edges off their own relationship.

When Nick phoned one night and asked if he could pop round, Jack didn't hesitate. He was happy to agree to anything that would help to build those all-essential bridges between them.

He had a pot of coffee ready when Nick arrived. He

showed him into the sitting room then poured them both a cup. Nick smiled when Jack handed him his cup.

'I see you've remembered that I prefer it black.'

'With two sugars,' Jack said easily, sitting down on a chair.

'Spot on.' Nick sat on the sofa. He took a sip of the coffee and nodded. 'It's very good, too. I am impressed.'

'I'm becoming quite domesticated,' Jack said, grinning.

Nick laughed. 'Your mother would have been delighted to hear that. She used to worry herself to death when you were at university in case you weren't eating properly.'

'I probably wasn't, but I survived.'

'Indeed you did.' Nick paused for a moment, then carried on. 'I'm really impressed with how well you're coping with Freddie, too. It can't have been easy for you, giving up your life in London, but you're doing a first-rate job with him.'

'Thanks,' Jack said, deeply touched because it was rare for his father to hand out a compliment. 'I appreciate you saying that.'

'It's no more than the truth.' Nick cleared his throat, then changed the subject. 'I wanted a word with you about a patient of mine, a ten-year-old-girl called Molly Dingle. She was involved in a horrific accident last year when she was on a school skiing trip. Another skier crashed into her and Molly suffered the most horrendous facial injuries—both eye sockets were shattered and her jaw was broken in two places.'

'Sounds grim,' Jack observed quietly. He'd seen those kind of injuries before and knew how difficult they were to put right.

'It was—very grim indeed. The surgeon managed to put everything back together but the results are less than perfect. Molly desperately needs another operation, but there's a waiting list and it could be over a year until it's her turn.

She's due to start secondary school in September, and she's terribly upset at the thought of the other kids making fun of her.'

'Kids can be very cruel,' Jack sympathised. 'Is there any chance of her going private?'

'No. Her father's a fisherman and her mum's a dinner lady at the junior school. It took them months to save enough to send her on the skiing trip, and private medicine is way beyond their means.' Nick pinned Jack with a look. 'That's why I was hoping you might be able to help.'

'You'd like me to take her on as a pro bono private patient?' Jack said slowly.

'Yes. It's the only way Molly will be able to get the treatment she needs in time for her to start at her new school after the summer.'

'I'm not in a position to set myself up in private practice just yet,' Jack pointed out. 'I've still got eighteen months of training to complete before I'm fully qualified.'

'I realise that,' Nick said impatiently. 'However, I know for a fact that you're more than capable of helping Molly.' He shrugged when Jack looked at him in surprise. 'I've spoken to a lot of people, and I can't count the number of folk who've told me that you're top of the league when it comes to this type of surgery. As far as I'm concerned, you'd do a better job than anyone else.'

'Thank you,' Jack said, somewhat stunned by the praise. He frowned as he considered the issues surrounding Molly's surgery. 'The main problem with this type of surgery when it involves a child is that they're still growing. Usually titanium plates and metals screws are used to hold the bones in place, but they can move as the child grows and that means further surgery is necessary. However, a technique has been developed recently which uses biodegradable implants. Over a period of time, the bone regrows and the implants disintegrate.'

'That would be marvellous!' Nick exclaimed. 'Have you seen this type of operation done?'

'Seen it and been trained in its methods.' Jack smiled. 'I managed to blag my way onto a training course in Germany last year where they pioneered the treatment. There were ten of us there and we spent three days learning how to operate the equipment.'

'How does it work?' Nick asked eagerly.

'The implants are made from a hydrocarbon material called poly-lactide. The plates are made to fit the patient's face and hold everything together. Holes are drilled in the bones and the plates are attached to them by means of plugs made from the same hydrocarbon material. An ultra-sound device is then used to weld the plugs to the bone.' He shrugged. 'It's highly effective. We were able to talk to a couple of patients who'd had the procedure done and the results were excellent.'

'And you think Molly could have this treatment?'

'I think so. There's a couple of hospitals in the UK that have the equipment now. I could find out if they would let us borrow it. Of course, a lot would depend on whether the management of St Piran's would agree to let us use the facilities there. It would have to be after normal working hours, of course, but I'm sure I can get Alex to back me up.'

'I'll write to the board,' Nick said immediately. 'There's a few favours I can call in if they refuse.'

Jack chuckled. 'I don't think they would dare refuse if you got involved as well.'

'There's strength in numbers,' Nick said with a wry smile. He drained the last of his coffee and stood up. 'Thanks, Jack.

I appreciate this, especially as I know I don't have any right to ask you for favours.'

'Of course you do!' Jack exclaimed, getting up. 'You're my father, and if you can't ask me for a favour I don't know who can. Anyway, I owe you for all the time you've given up to look after Freddie.'

'That's been a pleasure, not a chore,' Nick said firmly as he went to the door. He turned. 'I may not have been around as much as I should have been when you were growing up, Jack, but I always cared what happened to you.'

'I know you did,' Jack said with a lump in his throat. Stepping forward, he gave Nick a hug. 'Thanks, Dad. For everything.'

'Your mother would have been so proud of you, son,' Nick said huskily.

Jack saw him out, then went back to the sitting room and thought about what had happened. It had been easier than he'd thought it would be to smooth things over with his father. It was partly the fact that Nick seemed to have mellowed, but it was mainly the fact that his own attitude had changed. Becoming a father himself had made him reassess his priorities. Although his career would always be important to him, his family came first. He wanted to do what was right for them.

He also wanted to do what was right for Alison. That was equally important. Just for a second his mind went racing off as he imagined how his life could be. It would be so wonderful to have her at his side, to live with her and watch their children growing up. They could even have more children if she wanted them—he certainly did. He smiled. He would love a little girl with soft blonde hair and hazel eyes…

He sighed as he drove the images from his mind. It wasn't going to happen and he had to accept that. Alison had her own life, and it would be wrong for him to interfere at this stage when he had so little to offer her. Unless he was one hundred per cent sure that he could give her the commitment she deserved, he had to stay away from her. There could be no half-measures. It had to be all or nothing. Alison deserved nothing less.

CHAPTER FIFTEEN

THE last few days of March brought with them a storm. Rain lashed the countryside and a driving wind made getting around the town extremely difficult. Warnings were posted along the cliff top to warn the unwary about the dangers of going too close to the edge. Everyone at the surgery held their breath and hoped that any visitors would heed the warnings but, inevitably, there were casualties.

Nick and Dragan were called out to a walker who had been blown off the steps leading down to the beach and broken his leg. The man's wife had raised the alarm, and by the time they got there she was completely hysterical. When Nick phoned the surgery and asked for someone to go and attend to the woman while he and Dragan dealt with her husband, Alison immediately volunteered. Anything that might help to take her mind off her own problems was a welcome relief.

She parked in Mevagissey Road and went to find them. The sea was a churning mass of grey-green waves as it pounded the shore and she sincerely hoped that Nick and Dragan weren't down on the beach. She finally spotted them perched halfway up the steps. They were trying to attend to the injured man but his wife kept getting in the way.

Alison firmly ushered her out of the way while the two doctors got on with their job. She insisted that the woman should return to her car, but no sooner had they got there than the woman suffered an asthma attack. Alison found her inhaler in her pocket and got her sorted out, but she was relieved when the ambulance arrived to take the couple to hospital.

By the time the ambulance left it was lunchtime and she needed to collect Sam. She headed straight to the nursery, exclaiming in frustration when she discovered the road was blocked by an overturned lorry. Hunting her mobile phone out of her bag, she rang Carol, but there was no answer. Obviously, Carol had already left to collect her other charges from the nursery.

Alison phoned the nursery to warn them that she would be late, but the line was engaged, and it was still engaged when she tried another half a dozen times. By the time the road was clear she was over an hour late, and she could feel herself growing increasingly anxious. Sam would be terribly upset if he thought she'd forgotten him.

Trish answered the door when Alison rang the bell and she looked surprised to her. 'Did Sam forget something?'

'I don't think so,' Alison replied uncertainly, wondering what Trish meant. 'I'm sorry I'm so late, but a lorry had overturned and it held me up. Is Sam OK? He's not upset, is he?'

Trish blanched. 'Sam's not here. I thought you must have asked Carol to collect him.'

'I couldn't get hold of her,' Alison said, her heart racing. 'Why did you think he'd gone home with Carol? Did you see him leave with her?'

'No. I was in the quiet room when she arrived. Sam wasn't there when I got back, so I assumed she must have collected him, along with the other two she usually picks up.'

'Maybe she did,' Alison said, doing her best not to panic.

She took out her phone and rang Carol's number. 'Carol, it's Alison. Is Sam with you?'

Alison felt the floor tilt when the childminder told her that Sam wasn't there. Trish had gone to fetch Christine Galloway, the owner of the nursery; the pair of them looked worried to death when she told them that Sam wasn't at Carol's house either.

'We need to check that he isn't hiding somewhere,' Christine said quickly.

They searched every room, and even checked the garden, but there was no sign of him. Alison felt a wave of sickness envelop her when Christine told her that she was going to telephone the police. Where could Sam be? She glanced out of the window, feeling fear clutch her heart. It was pouring down with rain—what chance did a three-year-old have outside on his own in weather like this?

Jack heard about Sam when Lucy phoned to tell him. He had just left Theatre when the call came through, and it was like a bolt from the blue.

'What's happening now?' he demanded, his heart pounding in fear at the thought of the child going missing.

'The police have organised a search of the whole town. Dad and Ben have gone along to help,' Lucy explained. She gave a little sob. 'I can't bear to think what Alison must be going through at this moment.'

'Neither can I,' Jack said grimly. He thanked Lucy, then went to find Alex and explained that he needed to leave immediately. There was no way on earth that he could carry on working while Sam was missing.

He got changed, then drove straight to Alison's house. There was a police car parked outside, and a woman police officer answered the door when he rang the bell. Alison came rushing into the hall when she heard his voice. Jack didn't say a word as he pushed past the policewoman and took her in his arms. He rocked her to and fro as he felt the sobs that shook her.

'I'm so scared, Jack. I don't know what I'll do if anything happens to him…'

'Nothing is going to happen to him,' he said fiercely. He held her away from him and looked into her eyes. 'You have to believe that, sweetheart. Sam needs you to be strong for him.'

'I'm trying,' she whispered, her eyes brimming with tears.

'I know you are.' He kissed her gently on the mouth, then he let her go. 'I'm going to ask Lucy to look after Freddie so I can join the search party. We'll find him, Alison. Trust me. I won't let anything happen to Sam, I swear.'

He kissed her again, then left. He phoned Lucy as soon as he got home and arranged for her to have Freddie, then grabbed a waterproof jacket and went to join the search party. They'd been split into four teams so they could scour every part of the town. Jack went with his father and Ben while they searched the area around the nursery, but as the hours passed and there was still no sign of Sam he was starting to despair. He needed to find him for Alison's sake—needed to keep his promise and not let her down.

The group stopped for a break at seven p.m. The weather was atrocious and everyone was soaked to the skin. Jack shook his head when someone offered him a mug of soup. He didn't care how cold or wet he was. He just cared about Sam. He wandered a little way away from the rest of the group, heading to an area of rough land that was next on their list to be searched. There was a lot of bracken and gorse, and it tore at the legs of his jeans as he forced his way through it.

'Sam!' he shouted, cupping his hands round his mouth. 'Sam, can you hear me? It's Jack.'

He waited a moment, his ears straining against the roar of the wind, and felt his heart jerk when he heard a faint cry coming from off to his right. He plunged through the undergrowth, ripping his jeans and his skin as he raced towards the sound. When he caught sight of the small figure huddled beneath a huge gorse bush, he could have wept with relief.

Crouching down, he smiled at the little boy. 'Hi, there. How are you doing? Are you ready to go home and see your mummy?'

Sam reached out his arms and Jack lifted him up. He hugged him tight for a moment, then took off his coat and wrapped it around him. 'Over here,' he shouted, when he saw some of the others heading towards him. 'He's fine. He's just very cold and wet.'

A huge cheer erupted. Jack grinned as several people slapped him on the back. One of the police officers got straight on his radio and informed the other groups that Sam had been found, safe and sound. There was some talk of taking the child to hospital to be checked over, but Jack quashed that idea and his father backed him up. The best thing for the child was to be reunited with his mother as quickly as possible.

Alison came running out to meet them when they drew up outside the house. There was such happiness on her face that Jack couldn't help himself. He handed Sam to her, then bent and kissed her, uncaring that everyone was watching them. He didn't give a damn if the whole world knew how he felt. He loved her, and tonight had shown him that it was the only thing that really mattered.

'I love you,' he told her simply. 'Now, it's time you took Sam inside and gave him a bath.' He pressed a finger to her lips when she went to speak. 'He needs you. I can wait. My feelings for you aren't going to change, no matter how long it takes you to decide if you might be able to love me back one day.'

'I don't need time to decide that,' she said softly. Reaching up, she kissed him on the mouth. 'I love you, too, Jack. And what you've done tonight by finding Sam for me just makes me love you even more.'

There was so much that Jack wanted to say to her then but he couldn't be selfish and claim any more of her attention. He kissed her again, kissed Sam and hugged him too, then left. Ben offered to stay and check Sam over, but Nick insisted on driving him home. He smiled as he pulled up outside Jack's house.

'Don't worry about Freddie. I'll look after him tonight, and for however long you need to sort things out.'

'I love her, Dad,' Jack said simply, and Nick nodded.

'Then make sure she knows that. Life's too short to waste even a second of it. If it's Alison you want, then tell her that. OK?'

'OK,' Jack repeated, feeling a lump come to his throat because he would never have expected his father to understand.

He let himself in and took a shower, then made himself a cup of coffee, but didn't drink it. Those precious seconds were ticking away, and he didn't intend to let any more of them slip through his fingers. He was going back to Alison's house and he was going to tell her that he wanted to spend his life with her.

He took a deep breath as a feeling of certainty suddenly filled him. If there were problems that needed dealing with, they would deal with them together.

Alison took a last look at Sam, then tiptoed from the room. Ben had given the child a thorough examination and had decided that there was no reason to take him to hospital. A warm bath and plenty of cuddles were the best medicine he could prescribe, and she'd been more than happy to comply with those instructions. Although she hadn't managed to get the full story from Sam about how he had come to leave the nursery, it appeared that he had followed Carol out and then wandered off after she'd left.

She went downstairs, feeling herself trembling as the effects of the past few hours caught up with her. She'd been so scared that they might not find Sam, and it was such a relief to have him safely back home. Jack would never know how grateful she was to him for finding her precious child.

A smile softened the lines of strain around her mouth as she thought about what Jack had told her. There wasn't a doubt in her mind that he'd been sincere, and her heart overflowed with happiness at the thought. When she heard the doorbell ring, she hurried to answer it, knowing it would be him. He stepped into the hall and took her in his arms, and she sighed with pleasure. Now *everything* was right with her world.

He kissed her hungrily, then looked into her eyes. 'I love you so much. You do believe me, don't you?'

'Yes, I believe you.' She kissed him gently on the lips, then smiled at him. 'I love you, too, Jack.'

He swept her off her feet and twirled her round, laughing when she gasped. 'I'm sorry, but I'm so happy I think I might burst!'

Alison laughed with him. 'And I would hate that to happen. Apart from the fact that I like you just the way you are, think about the mess it would make.'

He chuckled as he set her back on her feet and kissed the tip of her nose. 'You're so wonderfully practical. No wonder I love you so much.'

'So long as you don't think I'm boring?'

'Boring?' He looked at her in amazement. 'You couldn't be boring if you tried! Whatever gave you that idea?'

'Well, I'm not at all like your usual girlfriends, am I? I'm not glamorous or rich, and I don't go to all sorts of exciting places,' she pointed out.

'No, thank heavens!' He steered her into the sitting room, sat down on the sofa and pulled her down onto his lap. He kissed her softly on the mouth, then smiled at her. 'You're nothing like the women I used to go out with. I wouldn't have fallen in love with you if you were.'

'Really?'

'Yes, really.' He sighed as he pulled her into his arms. 'I went out with them purely and simply because I knew I would *never* fall in love with them. It meant that I could focus on what was really important—my career.'

'So you don't hanker after those days?' she said quietly.

'Not at all. I enjoyed them at the time, but life moves on. I'm a very different person to who I was then.' He smiled ruefully. 'I doubt if you'd have fancied me if we'd met a couple of years ago.'

'Maybe not. I was still trying to come to terms with what had happened to me.'

'You mean your divorce?'

'That, and the fact that my confidence was at an all-time low.' She bit her lip, wondering if she should tell him about Sam's father, but it was important that he should know the truth.

'Sam's father left me when Sam was six months old. He'd been having an affair with a woman he worked with. I only found out about it by accident when I saw them together one day.' She shrugged. 'Gareth never tried to deny it. He said it was my fault it had happened.'

'Your fault? How did he work that out?' Jack demanded.

'Apparently I'd become boring after I'd had Sam, and let myself go.' She paused, but she needed to tell him everything. 'He said that he no longer fancied me because I was so fat and ugly.'

Jack swore under his breath as he drew her to him. 'I wish I could have five minutes alone with him. How dare he say such terrible things to you?'

'I can see now that it was just a way to excuse his own behaviour. Gareth never liked to think he was at fault, so he blamed me. It was the same throughout our marriage. He was always finding fault with what I did. Even though I no longer had any feelings for him by the time we divorced, it hit me hard. It completely eroded my self-esteem.'

'You are a beautiful woman and a very special person, too,' Jack stated emphatically. 'I've never met anyone like you before. You're so warm and giving, so capable and so gorgeous—'

'Stop!' she begged, placing her hand over his mouth. 'My head is going to be so swollen I'll not be able to get out of that door if you keep on showering me with compliments.'

Jack grinned. 'We certainly don't want that happening. I have plans that involve us both leaving this room and going upstairs to somewhere more comfortable.'

Alison shivered at the image that sprang to her mind. She could picture her and Jack walking up the stairs to her bedroom… She blanked out the rest, knowing that it would be impossible to concentrate if she got too carried away. 'As I said, it took me a long time to find myself again. That's why I was so scared when I realised the effect you had on me. I was terrified of being hurt again the way I'd been hurt before.'

'I will never hurt you, Alison.' He pressed her hand to his heart and held it there. 'I swear on my life that I shall do my best to protect you and make you happy. You and Sam, of course.'

'Thank you.' Tears welled to her eyes, because there was no doubt that he was telling her the truth. She kissed him on the mouth, then snuggled into his arms, enjoying the fact that she could do so. There were no barriers between them now, and she was free to show him her love any way she chose.

Jack brushed his mouth across her hair. 'If it's confession time then I have a confession, too. I tried desperately not to fall in love with you. Even when I realised it had happened, despite my attempts to stop it, I still couldn't tell you how I felt. That's why I stayed away. I didn't want to risk telling you that I loved you.'

'Because of Freddie?'

'Yes. He needs so much of my time and attention. It just didn't seem fair to involve you in my life at the moment.'

'I thought it was because you weren't interested in me,' she admitted. 'Especially when I saw you with Alex Ross that day.'

'Really?' He groaned. 'I wish I'd known that. Alex had asked me to meet her in Rock so we could discuss this new clinic she's involved with. There's nothing going on between us, Alison, I promise you.'

'I believe you.' She tipped back her head and looked at him. 'I would never make you choose between me and Freddie. He needs you, and I'm happy to wait for however long it takes.'

'Thank you.' He kissed her gently. 'I don't want to wait, though. I want us to be together now, not at some point in the future. I need you beside me, Alison. If there are problems, I know we can solve them if we do it together—you, me, Sam and Freddie.'

Alison wound her arms around his neck. Jack was right.

There was no problem too big that they couldn't solve together. Her heart overflowed with love when he set her on her feet and led her to the stairs. This was the start of a whole new life for all of them.

EPILOGUE

It was the day of Maggie and Adam's wedding, and it appeared that the whole of Penhally Bay had turned out to wish them well. The local church was packed as the couple made their vows. Maggie looked lovely in a simple white dress and carrying a bouquet of spring flowers, and Adam looked so handsome in his dark suit. They made a perfect couple and everyone was thrilled for them.

Alison sat at the back of the church with Jack and the boys, and cried throughout the service. It was just so beautiful and so moving, especially in view of what had happened to her. Jack took her hand and held it tightly, and she knew that he felt as emotional as she did, and for the same reasons, too. They were so in tune with one another that it was hard to imagine being without him now, and she didn't try. Jack was part of her life now and she was part of his—they were inseparable.

Maggie and Adam had decided not to have a reception. As they had explained, they wanted to be on their own more than anything else, and everyone had understood. Alison followed the rest of the party outside as everyone went to wave them off. When Maggie tossed her bouquet to the crowd, Alison automatically reached for it, but missed. It wasn't until a great cheer erupted that she discovered Jack had caught it.

He grinned as he handed it to her. 'This is for you.'

'Thank you.' Alison laughed as she took it from him, then gasped when he dropped to one knee in front of her. 'What are you doing?'

'What do you think?'

He gave her a wicked grin, then called Freddie over and whispered something to him. The little boy solemnly felt in his pocket and drew out a velvet-covered box, which Jack then gave to Sam. Alison's heart was racing as her son proudly handed the box to her.

'Alison Myers, will you do me the honour of becoming my wife?' Jack said as everyone held their breath.

'I…er…um…' Alison tailed off and swallowed. Her hands were shaking so hard that she could barely open the box, and when she finally managed it, she gasped again. The ring was gorgeous, a diamond solitaire in a delicate platinum setting.

'I don't want to rush you, my love, but I'm starting to get cramp,' Jack said, sounding slightly nervous. 'Please, say you'll marry me and put me out of my misery.'

'Yes,' she whispered, then took a deep breath and repeated her answer so that everyone could hear her. 'Yes, I'll marry you, Jack!'

All the guests went wild, but Alison was barely aware of what was going on around them. Jack stood up and kissed her, then took hold of the boys' hands.

'Right, let's go and see if Granddad would mind looking after you two for a couple of hours.' He smiled at Alison, a smile that was filled with promise. 'Alison and I have things to do this afternoon.'

He led the children through the crowd, pausing to accept congratulations along the way. His father was talking to Lucy, and they both turned and smiled when they saw him approaching.

'Granddad!' Freddie suddenly shouted, catching sight of Nick. He and Sam went racing off, but Jack stopped dead. He couldn't believe that Freddie had spoken at last—yet wasn't it fitting that it should have happened today?

A wave of happiness enveloped him as he looked back at Alison. He'd had so many doubts when he had come back to Penhally Bay, but it had worked out far better than he had hoped. Not only did he have a son he adored, he had found the woman he wanted to spend the rest of his life with. He had to be the luckiest man alive!

Dear Reader,

I was delighted to be asked to take part in this series. I have been writing for Harlequin Books for twenty years now, and I can honestly say that they have been some of the best years of my life. And it is always lovely to work closely with fellow writers.

My book is number four in the Penhally series, and I have to confess that I have a soft spot for my hero, Jack Tremayne. Jack was always the black sheep of the family, the one who pushed all the boundaries and refused to conform. When he returns to Penhally Bay with his small son, Freddie, he isn't sure if he is doing the right thing. He desperately needs his family's support to help him cope as a single dad, but will he be able to make his peace with his father? What Jack doesn't anticipate is the impact Alison Myers will have on his life.

Helping Jack and Alison fall in love was a real pleasure. The fact that I was able to set their story against the wonderful Cornish background of Penhally Bay was a bonus. Don't forget to look out for the rest of the books in this series. I've already placed my order!

Jennifer

www.jennifer-taylor.com

Welcome to Penhally Bay!

Nestled on the rugged Cornish coast in England is the picturesque town of Penhally—a warm, bustling community with sandy beaches and breathtaking landscapes. It is the lucky tourist who stumbles upon this little haven.

But now Harlequin® Medical Romance™ is giving readers the unique opportunity to visit this fictional coastal town through our brand-new sixteen-book continuity. Welcome to a town where fishing boats bob in the bay, surfers wait expectantly for the waves, friendly faces line the cobbled streets and romance flutters on the Cornish sea breeze.

We introduce you to Penhally Bay Surgery, where you can meet the team led by caring and commanding Dr. Nick Tremayne. Each book will bring you an emotional, tempting romance—from Mediterranean heroes to a sheikh with a guarded heart. There's royal scandal that leads to marriage for a baby's sake, and handsome playboys are tamed by their blushing brides. Top-notch city surgeons win adoring smiles from the community, and little miracle babies will warm your hearts. But that's not all....

With Penhally Bay you get double the reading pleasure—each book also follows the life of damaged hero Dr. Nick Tremayne. His story, a tale of lost love and the torment of forbidden romance, will pierce your heart. Dr. Nick's unquestionable, unrelenting skill would leave any patient happy in the knowledge that she's in safe hands, and is a testament to the ability and dedication of all the staff at Penhally Bay Surgery. Come in and meet them for yourself....